Robyn's mind was whirling

A marriage that was not a marriage...to this man? Everything within her recoiled from such a cold-blooded relationship with Julian Lassiter.

She was so outraged that he should suggest it that she barely heard the conditions he was laying down.

"I doubt you'd find a better man to father your child if you looked for a million years," he finally concluded.

"That is a matter of opinion, Mr. Lassiter," she said caustically.

An angry flush suffused his face. "For heaven's sake! What more do you want?"

Pride drew her to her feet in haughty disdain of his humiliating proposition. "I'll tell you what I want, Mr. Lassiter. I want to choose for myself."

EMMA DARCY nearly became an actress until her fiancé declared he preferred to attend the theater *with* her. She became a wife and mother. Later she took up oil painting—unsuccessfully, she remarks. Then, she tried architecture, designing the family home in New South Wales. Next came romance writing—"the hardest and most challenging of all the activities," she confesses.

Books by Emma Darcy

HARLEQUIN PRESENTS

1020—THE WRONG MIRROR
1033—THE ONE THAT GOT AWAY
1048—STRIKE AT THE HEART
1080—THE POSITIVE APPROACH
1103—MISTRESS OF PILLATORO
1151—ALWAYS LOVE
1177—A PRICELESS LOVE

HARLEQUIN ROMANCE

2900—BLIND DATE
2941—WHIRLPOOL OF PASSION

EMMA DARCY

the aloha bride

Harlequin Books

TORONTO • NEW YORK • LONDON
AMSTERDAM • PARIS • SYDNEY • HAMBURG
STOCKHOLM • ATHENS • TOKYO • MILAN

Harlequin Presents first edition September 1989
ISBN 0-373-11199-1

Original hardcover edition published in 1988
by Mills & Boon Limited

CHAPTER ONE

THEY faced each other across the baggage carousel at Maui Airport. Robyn could hardly avoid noticing him. His clothes alone would have made him stand out from the crowd. All the people around him favoured the casual tourist gear that proclaimed they were either arriving for a holiday or on their way home from one. He wore a suit—dark grey and obviously custom-tailored to fit a physique that looked very well proportioned in the strong male mould.

He was tall and dark. His head was half turned towards the flaps through which the luggage would soon emerge, but his profile confirmed that he had a finely balanced arrangement of features—quite compellingly attractive—although he was a good ten years older than herself. Robyn judged he was closer to forty than thirty. She wondered what business he had on this tropical Hawaiian island.

Robyn was sure it would be business and not pleasure. She had a lot of experience at appraising people. For several years she had worked in a travel agency before going into business for herself, putting together tour packages that had sold well and proved very popular. She had an instinct for what people wanted, even when they couldn't express it themselves. And one comprehensive look at the man in the grey suit was enough to spell it out to her.

He was trouble.

He held a Qantas cabin-bag—the kind Robyn knew to be issued only to first-class passengers. And he would want everything first class...the type who knew the chairman of the board of directors if he didn't get precisely what he expected. Wealth...success...intrinsic self-assurance...his whole bearing and demeanour embodied those qualities.

Even the stylish cut of his thick black hair hadn't dared to move a millimetre, despite the gusty winds that had almost lifted people off their feet as they had disembarked on the Maui tarmac.

A musing little smile was still hovering on Robyn's lips when he turned his head and looked straight at her.

And she couldn't look away!

The strong, masculine lines of his face were so striking that only a privileged ancestry could have bequeathed them. His eyes held hers totally captive as they bored into her, causing her heart to jolt with almost sickening force.

Robyn was suddenly very conscious of her windswept hair and the practical simplicity of her clothes: a matching top and skirt in a light polyester mix that didn't crush but was hardly classy with its blue and white print of tropical fish.

His gaze flicked down her figure, noting the full thrust of her breasts against the softly clinging material, the womanly roundness of her hips, and the smooth, long line of her legs. The sharp rake of his appraisal dug furrows of heat into her skin, and Robyn felt her whole body flushing as his gaze returned to hers. She instantly recognised the simmering look in his eyes—a challenging glitter of sexual speculation that said he found her physically attractive—enough to entertain the fantasy of what she might be like in bed—but no interest at all in her as a person.

His mouth curved into a cynical little smile, mocking himself and dismissing her. He looked away.

The carousel began to move.

Robyn stared blindly at it, feeling ridiculously shaken. It wasn't the first time a man had appraised her like that. Why should she be so unnerved by it? Or feel belittled by his dismissal? She had known from the first glance at him that he was out of her class. He was certainly not the kind of man she was used to meeting and mixing with, not on first-name terms. And she was finished with men, anyway!

She supposed she should be grateful that Larry had let her down before they were married, instead of after. But she didn't feel grateful. Robyn had suffered a long string of let-downs in her life, but Larry's desertion was the bitterest one of all. No more, she thought determinedly. From now on she would stick to being a career-person, pure and simple.

After all, she had seen the results of marriage on her mother and both her older sisters, and it was probably very fortunate that she was still single. There were no innocent children left to suffer through the emotional debris of a divorce.

How easy it was to make a terrible mistake! She had thought Larry so steadfast and reliable. They had been friends for such a long time, yet she hadn't really known him at all. When she had seen him with that girl—a petite, bubbly girl who was so unlike Robyn it was almost insulting that Larry should fall so passionately in love with her—there had been nothing she could do or say but let him go.

She had been alone before. Most of her life. And better to stay that way, Robyn thought grimly. She flashed a resentful glance at the man opposite her as he lifted an expensive leather suitcase from the carousel. He moved away through the crowd without so much as a backward glance at her.

Gone out of her life. Just like Larry.

But she was not going to feel miserable and morose, Robyn resolved firmly. Here she was, on her way to one of the best hotels in the world, situated on one of the most beautiful islands in the Pacific Ocean, with a whole week of tropical luxury in front of her... and so what if it should have been her honeymoon! She had paid for it and she was going to enjoy it!

The sight of her suitcase buoyed up the sense of anticipation that Robyn clung on to in order to keep other thoughts at bay. She hauled the heavy bag off the carousel and made her way out of the terminal.

Her pulse skipped a beat when she saw the man in the grey suit ahead of her. He was standing on the edge of the footpath, scanning the row of taxis on the far side of the road. Robyn quickly averted her gaze, inwardly squirming at the thought of his catching her eye again. She kept her head down until she had passed behind him. When she looked up to check where she should go to catch a shuttle to the hotel, her heart stopped dead.

It was going to happen. Robyn saw it in a flash—the fork-lift chuntering along with its load of crates; its driver shouting out behind him to one of his friends; the little old lady in the middle of the road trying to pull free the strap which had fouled the smooth running of the castors on her suitcase—neither of them was watching!

Robyn's feet moved even as she yelled for the driver to stop. But the accident was still going to happen—

inevitably—unless she did something! She dropped her bag and ran. Her shout towards the driver had alerted the woman to the danger she was in, but she stood frozen in the face of oncoming disaster. The driver screamed at her to get out of the way as he frantically applied the brakes, but the old lady just stared, completely mesmerised by the tower of crates bearing down on her.

No time for gentle persuasion! Robyn charged rugby-style, grabbing the old lady around the shoulders and using her own momentum to haul her forward. She felt the fork-lift brush past her and she almost stumbled out of sheer fright, but they were safe, out of harm's way. She glanced over her shoulder to see the lumbering machine push the shabby brown suitcase a couple of feet before grinding to a halt.

The driver, who looked to be part-Philippine and part-Japanese, leapt out of his seat in a flurry of concern, apologising profusely. The old lady was too dazed to take anything in, and his excitability was not helping matters. Robyn firmly instructed him to retrieve the suitcase and see that it wasn't damaged. He picked it up, brushed it down, then carried it after them as Robyn helped the woman to the pavement.

The hand that clutched her arm was very shaky. Once they were at the entrance to the airport terminal, the old lady faltered to a halt and took several deep breaths. 'Thank you...I wasn't looking...the strap was caught...and somehow I couldn't move...'

'Not to worry,' Robyn soothed. 'Everything's fine now.'

The driver set the suitcase beside them, obviously anxious to be finished with the incident, gabbled another apology and hurried back to the fork-lift.

The woman looked up at Robyn in grateful relief. She was a dumpy little person—anyone's grandmother—and her eyes suddenly filled with tears.

'Oh...the pain...the pain,' she gasped.

Frightened that the shock of the near-accident had brought on a heart attack, Robyn instinctively tightened the hold of her supporting arm, ready to catch the woman if she should start to fall. She wondered if there was any facility for emergency treatment here. Surely an airport had some kind of medical aid on quick call.

'Where do you hurt?' she asked anxiously.

'Not me. It's you.' Her kindly face puckered in concern. 'The agony...I'm so sorry for you, my dear. For what you're going to suffer.'

'Me?' Robyn was totally bewildered. 'I'm fine! I'm not hurt at all. The machine didn't even touch me.'

'I don't mean now,' came the even more perplexing reply. 'For what's going to happen. Sometimes I can tell, you see. When I touch people. I can feel what's going to happen.'

Robyn broke into nervous laughter, a little shaken by the old lady's intensity. 'Well, I hope you're wrong this time.'

The knowing old eyes dilated with anguish. 'I wish I was. But for some reason, I never am. The greatest sadness...' Her gaze shifted vaguely to a point over Robyn's shoulder. Then her expression lightened, a pleased smile curving her mouth as her eyes refocused on Robyn. '...but then the greatest happiness. Yes...may God give you the strength to carry through.'

She released Robyn's arm and patted her hand comfortingly. 'It will be all right. Yes, it will be all right when you marry.'

Marry! No likelihood of that any more, Robyn thought sharply, but she did not bother voicing her sentiments on that sore subject. Perhaps the old lady did have some kind of psychic gift and she had picked up vibrations of the past—the planned marriage to Larry—but she was right off beam about the future. And, as far as any sadness over being jilted was concerned, she would survive that. She had survived everything else.

Robyn dismissed the whole prediction with a firm mental shrug. 'Are you OK now?' she asked, forcing things back to practical reality.

'Oh, yes! Thank you. You've been so kind. And I am so glad you will be happy.' She picked up the offending strap, threw Robyn one more grateful smile and started off into the airport terminal with the suitcase rolling smoothly beside her.

'Wait!' Robyn called. It was not every day that one met a person who claimed to be a clairvoyant, and Robyn could not resist one tell-tale question...one that would establish beyond a doubt just how much the prediction was worth.

The old lady turned around enquiringly.

She looked so kind and benevolent that Robyn felt half ashamed of her cynicism. She didn't want to give offence—indeed, she expected a vague, indeterminate reply—so she smiled as she put the question. 'Before you go, you'd better tell me who I'm supposed to marry.'

Surprise flitted over the old lady's face. 'Why, that's obvious. The man behind you, of course,' she said unequivocally, then smiled her blessing and went on her way.

She was swallowed into a milling crowd of people and disappeared, leaving Robyn too stunned by the positive reply even to think of pursuing the matter any further.

Of course, she didn't believe the old lady. The whole thing was ridiculous.

But an odd, crawly feeling ran down Robyn's spine as she turned to look at the man designated as her husband-to-be.

CHAPTER TWO

THERE was only one man who could rightfully be called 'behind her', and Robyn breathed a sigh of relief that he was facing the other way. If he had seen the near-accident or paid any attention to the resolution of the matter, he gave no indication of it. He was in the act of hailing a taxi from the waiting rank.

Of all the men in the world the old lady could have chosen, the man in the grey suit could not have been further from the mark, Robyn thought with savage irony. They would never mix, let alone match! Besides, a man like him would hardly be unattached except through choice. And he wasn't about to choose her for a lifelong partner.

His dismissal of her still stung.

Perhaps the old lady had somehow tuned in on that moment when they had faced each other across the carousel. But it had meant nothing. An unwilling attraction...short, sharp, finished. Robyn had to admit that the impact of it had left her shaken, in a way she had never been shaken before, but a man like him would only be trouble. She had figured that out before he had even looked at her.

The taxi pulled into the kerb in front of him, carefully positioned so that he hardly had to move. The driver alighted and Robyn noted his automatic response to the innate authority of the man...the respectful greeting and handling of his luggage.

Currying favour for a big fat tip, Robyn thought cynically, and undoubtedly he would get it. These people knew their mark.

A burst of pride in her own worth prodded Robyn forward as the man rounded the taxi to the opened passenger door. Why should she hang back because of him? She had to collect her suitcase which she had abandoned in running to the old lady's aid, and she could tap the taxi-driver's local knowledge at the same time.

'Could you please tell me where I might find the shuttle to the Hyatt-Regency Hotel?' she asked, keeping her gaze fixed on the driver and consciously averted from the man in the grey suit.

She had checked the prices before she left Australia—thirty-six dollars for a taxi, eight dollars fifty for the shuttle. Even if she was intent on indulging herself in the holiday of a lifetime, she was not going to throw money away on pointless extravagance.

The driver nodded to a parking area beyond the pedestrian crossing. 'Just over the other side. But you'll probably have a longish wait for it. It's usually a forty-minute run to the Ka'anapali beach resort, dependent on traffic, and the shuttle left here after the last flight half an hour ago. Next trip out won't be for another hour.'

'Thank you,' Robyn sighed, disappointed at the unavoidable delay. She picked up her suitcase, thinking she might as well go back inside the terminal and buy a cup of coffee.

'I'm going to the Hyatt—if you'd like to share my taxi.'

She looked up, not only surprised by the man's offer, but by his accent. Despite his Qantas bag, she hadn't expected him to be an Australian like herself. She had not met or heard one fellow countryman during her three days' stopover at Waikiki Beach in Honolulu. Americans, Japanese, the occasional French or German national, but no Australians.

He stood at the passenger door, looking at her over the roof of the car, and there was an encouraging half-smile on his face that invited . . . yet there was a look of hard reserve in his eyes that suggested he gave the invitation against his better judgement.

All Robyn's instincts recoiled from accepting the offer. 'It's very kind of you . . .' she said, mentally looking for excuses to forgo any real meeting with him. He was too disturbingly attractive. She was trying to get over a major disturbance in her life. She certainly didn't need another. 'It's more than I want to spend,' she added firmly.

'Be my guest,' he said in a casually autocratic tone of voice. 'I saw what you did for the old lady. One good turn deserves another. And this is mine.'

Taking her acceptance completely for granted, he strode back around the car, took her suitcase from her hand while Robyn was still too startled to protest, passed it over to the taxi-driver, opened the door for her, and gave her elbow a prompting push. She stepped into the car without any real volition of her own, and the moment she had settled on to the back seat he closed the door.

Resentment and fear welled up inside Robyn. He had taken control from her, decisively, and with the ease of a man born to command. It had all happened so fast and unexpectedly that she had been robbed of the will to resist. The urge to bolt out of the car while she still had the chance had her reaching for the door-handle, but reason insisted that such a move would be utterly stupid.

He had made a generous offer. It would be silly not to accept it. Sharing a forty-minute trip didn't mean anything. The man didn't care about her any more than she cared about him. This was just a bit of consideration for a fellow traveller—impulsively given—and should be treated as such; nothing more. And it would save her the shuttle-fare.

Robyn settled back, determined to relax and enjoy the comfortable ride. Her arrogantly forceful benefactor opened the other passenger door and slid on to the seat beside her. The moment he shut his door, Robyn's defensive instincts leapt straight to red alert. For the first time in her life, she felt her rigidly kept personal space invaded.

He wasn't touching her—there was a good foot of distance between them—yet his presence in this enclosed car seemed to exude danger; so much so that Robyn's skin broke out in goose-bumps.

It was stepping from the heat into this air-conditioned taxi, she argued fiercely to herself. Or she was being absurdly over-sensitive because of the old lady's prediction.

And with that last thought came a rush of hot embarrassment that whipped the chill from her skin and replaced it with a burning flush. The best defence was attack, her mind screamed. Her eyes darted accusingly at her companion and the words snapped off her tongue.

'Did you hear what she told me?'

'Pardon?' His eyes were hazel-green, deep-set and thickly lashed. They were tired, uninterested.

'The lady I helped,' Robyn persisted, unable to leave it alone until the horrible suspicion was completely allayed.

His gaze took in the hectic colour in Robyn's cheeks, then returned to the agitated probe of her wide blue eyes.

'I really don't know what you're talking about. I'm sorry. My mind was on other things, Miss...?'

'Walker. Robyn Walker,' she supplied in a rush of relief.

'Julian Lassiter.' He nodded, but didn't offer his hand. His rather hard mouth softened into a half-smile of dry amusement. 'If you're worried that my offer of a lift was the initial step to making some kind of pass at you, Miss Walker, please relax. I'm beyond the stage of running after everything that wears a skirt. And anyone who applied the label of misogynist to me would not be too far wrong. I choose any companion I have very carefully.'

Robyn laughed in sheer nervous reaction. At least he didn't know he was supposed to marry her. And certainly a man who disliked women as much as he claimed to was hardly likely to be any more interested in marriage than she was.

'Well, that was a fair old put-down, Mr Lassiter, but I'm grateful for it. A girl can't be too careful these days. And now we both know where we are,' she rattled off, trying her hardest to feel more at ease with him.

'I didn't mean to be uncomplimentary. Or uncivil,' he amended quickly.

His eyes made a quick, appreciative appraisal of the chic cut of her blonde hair, the attractive way it was shaped to her head, sweeping softly across her forehead and cleverly curving in to complement the line of cheek and jaw. She had a slightly long nose and a very generous, full-lipped mouth—some people had called it sensual—but both features suited the strongly defined bone-structure of her face; and the wide spacing of her cornflower-blue eyes gave her a very individual look. Her complexion was good and the sun-filled days on Oahu had blessed her with a light golden tan.

'You won't have any trouble finding yourself a man,' he observed, giving her a sardonic smile. 'But mark me off the list. I don't have the time, the inclination, the need...'

'I'm not looking for a man,' Robyn cut in, bristling at the implication.

'No?'

The dry mockery in his voice instantly recalled the humiliating fact that he had caught her staring at him.

'I would have thought that most women who came alone on vacation were on the look-out for someone to...share the pleasures,' he drawled meaningfully.

Robyn burned. 'You really shouldn't assign your own motives to everyone else, Mr Lassiter.'

It startled him out of his cynical complacency. He gave a short, harsh laugh, then sliced her an amused look that held a deliberately provocative glint. 'I'm not here to have a holiday, Miss Walker. But if there were anyone who could change my mind, it might be you.'

How Robyn kept her composure she didn't know— the blatant condescension of the man had her seething— but she returned his look with a flat, challenging stare. 'Am I supposed to be flattered by that remark?'

'It's more than I would say to most women,' he replied, and for the first time there was flicker of real interest in his eyes, a spark of curiosity. 'But then most women with your physical attributes wouldn't put themselves at risk to save someone from injury.'

'That's ridiculous! Anyone who saw it happening would have done the same,' Robyn protested.

His eyes mocked her assertion. 'You could have been hurt yourself. Your vacation ruined,' he pointed out.

'I hardly had time to think of that,' Robyn replied curtly, disliking his attitude so intensely that she was tempted to get out of the car and leave him to it.

'No, of course not,' he murmured, as if her reply had satisfied whatever question had been in his mind. A shuttered look came over his face and he turned away, withdrawing into himself.

It was positively perverse of her to feel a strong stab of disappointment, particularly after the sharp antagonism he had aroused. And she hated him ignoring her, as if she weren't beside him at all. It was even more diminishing than his first dismissal.

Robyn wished he hadn't spoken to her at all. She thought again of getting out of the car, but pride held her there. She was not going to let him think he intimidated her in any shape or form.

Their taxi-driver had been haggling with some official, but when he finally took his place behind the wheel he threw them a happy grin. '*Aloha!* Welcome to Maui!'

'What does *aloha* actually mean?' Robyn asked him impulsively. At least the taxi-driver recognised her as a person worth talking to, and any distraction from Julian Lassiter's insulting withdrawal was helpful in this situation.

'*Aloha?* It means many things. Mostly it is used as a greeting...hello...goodbye...but it can also mean love, mercy, compassion or pity. Among the old Hawaiians it was only used as a special greeting to very dear friends. It actually meant "Eye to eye, face to face, I greet you and give to you my peace, in fact, the very breath of life".'

'That's beautiful,' Robyn murmured, wishing that somehow the value of the word had not been diminished by the casual use that was now made of it. She silently recited the words over to herself, wanting to remember them.

The driver carried on with a cheerful spiel about this most beautiful island of the Hawaiian group as he drove out of the airport and joined the line of traffic heading west.

Robyn tried to concentrate on what he was saying, but she found it difficult to tear her thoughts from the man beside her. Julian Lassiter could not have made it any clearer that he was not interested in any kind of involvement with her, yet she could not repress her own awareness of him. It was very unsettling.

Whenever the driver pointed out a feature of the island on Julian's side of the car, Robyn found herself using the opportunity for a covert study of the man.

His skin was pale, as if he spent too much time indoors. His eyes were hooded, and more times than not he didn't bother to turn his head to see what there was to see. Although his hands lay loosely on his powerfully muscled thighs, she sensed a hard-coiled tension in him that tore at her nerves.

The driver tossed her an encouraging grin. 'Ask me any questions you like. I know everything about Maui.'

They were driving past lush fields of sugar-cane, and Robyn forced herself to find a question. It seemed rude not to show some interest. 'The large mounds of rocks everywhere . . . do they have any special significance?'

'Lots of volcanic rocks here,' came the cheerful answer. 'They have to be put somewhere when we clear the ground for cultivation.'

Robyn had thought vaguely of some ancient religious meaning, and felt like an idiot for not realising the obvious. She lapsed into silence again. She had shown her ignorance. Julian Lassiter could ask the questions from now on. But a surreptitious glance at him told her that none would be forthcoming. He showed no sign of having heard a word.

He had a gold ring on the third finger of his left hand!

They joined the coastal road and the driver launched into another tourist spiel. It all floated over Robyn's head. She had been swamped by a mad jumble of emotions that shocked her with their intensity.

Why should it upset her that Julian Lassiter was married? It wasn't as if she liked the man. Even if he was attractive physically, he certainly didn't have an attractive personality. He hadn't done or said a single thing to win her good opinion, except offer her a lift in his taxi. And he had made her pay for that in terms of heartburn. She hadn't been able to enjoy the trip at all, which she would have done in the shuttle by herself.

Married!

So much for the old lady's prediction!

Not that Robyn had ever believed it. Or wanted it to come true. You simply couldn't trust men. She had found that out with Larry. And she had been an absolute fool to let Julian Lassiter dominate her thoughts for as long as he had.

She willed her whole concentration on what the taxi-driver was saying, determined not to miss another thing. After all, it was unlikely that she would ever indulge herself in such a holiday again. Honeymoons were a once-in-a-lifetime extravagance.

'Only three more miles...'

Robyn heard the words with relief. The sooner she was away from Julian Lassiter and back on her own, the better. She had learnt to cope with being alone many years ago, long before Larry came into her life and held out the unfulfilled promise of a real and lasting companionship. Ever since she was seven years old...

Her mind drifted back to when her father had deserted the family; the frightening loss of any sense of security; the subsequent neglect while her mother had chased another husband; the violent temper and heavy hand of her first stepfather and the relief when he had died of a heart attack; another round of neglect and then...then avoiding the hot eyes and much more insidious hand of her second stepfather.

Her mother was one of those women who had to have a man—any man—to give them identity and purpose in life. Her children had simply come with the territory and were more a trouble than anything else; particularly Robyn...so much younger than her two sisters, the afterthought, the nuisance...the one that nobody wanted to bother with.

Robyn could see her sisters repeating the pattern. And if she herself had married Larry...but she was not going to think about Larry any more! She had been a fool to consider marriage at all. Hadn't she proved she was eminently capable of standing on her own two feet ever since she had left school? Dependent on no one! Of course she could go it alone!

'...We're passing through the outskirts of Lahaina, which used to be a whaling village and also the seat of government for all of Hawaii. Very historic,' the driver informed them. 'You will enjoy visiting it. So many interesting things to see: the old courthouse, the harbour, the banyan tree that spreads over a whole town block...'

Robyn dragged her mind back to the immediate present and forced herself to concentrate on the scenery. As they travelled beyond the village, she noticed that the roadside was planted with hibiscus bushes and bougainvillaea.

Palm trees were suddenly plentiful. They drove past the lush green fairways of a golf course and turned into the resort complex where a row of multi-storeyed hotels curved around the beach-front.

The Hyatt-Regency on the far left of the row looked impressive enough to satisfy Robyn's critical eye. Whether the hotel would live up to its reputation she would soon discover for herself. The taxi pulled up beside a wide pavement where a workmanlike reception desk handled the practical details of parking cars and assigning bellboys to arriving guests.

Robyn constructed a polite smile and turned to Julian Lassiter. 'Thank you for the lift. I appreciate the time it saved me.'

'My pleasure,' he murmured, the words a mere automatic response. His gaze only stabbed a brief acknowledgement at her before turning expectantly to the hotel entrance.

The driver skipped around the car to open Robyn's door and she climbed out into the free heat of the afternoon with a surge of relief. She barely had time to stretch her long legs when another stranger virtually accosted her, his face faintly creased into a smile of surprise and welcoming pleasure.

'Julian! Why didn't you tell me? How wonderful to see you with a woman again!' He threw an astonished look over the bonnet of the taxi to her taciturn companion before turning back at Robyn. 'And he'd convinced me he was a perpetual widower.'

His eyes ran assessingly over her and grew in warmth as Robyn struggled to absorb another shock. If Julian Lassiter was a widower...

'*Aloha,* indeed!' the newcomer said in a tone of empathic welcome. 'And I couldn't be more delighted to see my brother...with such a beautiful companion.'

'Davey...' There was a touch of exasperation in Julian Lassiter's voice. 'Miss Walker was merely sharing my taxi from the airport.'

Davey's face fell, then rearranged itself in sober apology as he turned to face Robyn fully. 'What a shame! I really was hoping for some kind of diversion, and you looked so much like a ray of sunshine.' But the warmth in his eyes became more distant as he appraised her again...the assessment more calculating this time. 'You are...very beautiful.'

'It's kind of you to say so,' Robyn smiled, trying to relieve the awkwardness of the moment, and thinking that he could certainly do with some sunshine.

His skin was so white it was almost translucent, making the rich auburn of his hair and his light green eyes quite startling in contrast. She did not have to be psychic to realise that here was a man who was either suffering some serious illness or had done so in the very recent past.

She would never have guessed he was Julian Lassiter's brother, yet his features held the same cut and strength. The likeness was even more apparent when the two men faced each other: the same height, the same kind of build, the same air of inner power under control.

Their greeting was curiously tense: Julian eyeing his brother sharply, Davey suddenly looking strained, despite the smile still lingering on his lips. Robyn couldn't help but eavesdrop, although she had stepped back to distance herself from the meeting. The taxi-driver was chatting to the bellhop who had rolled his trolley forward

for the luggage, and there was nothing else for Robyn
to do but wait until it was loaded.

'How did it go?' Davey asked.

'Not good. Your mother wants you home.'

The half-smile twisted. 'You know what she'd do,
Julian.'

'Yes, I know.'

'I couldn't stand it.'

'She loves you,' Julian said softly. 'You're the only
child she has, Davey. She needs to...'

'It's my life...' he said with low ferocity, then, on a
lighter, mocking note, '...what's left of it.'

'I promised to bear the message, that's all. I stand by
your choice, Davey.'

'Thanks, Julian.' The mild smile came back. 'I always
counted on you.'

'Can't help myself,' Julian retorted, and seemed to be
mocking himself.

Davey clapped him on the shoulder, but Robyn noticed that after a moment's pause the white fingers dug
in and squeezed, revealing emotion that wasn't spoken.
They were close, even though the way Julian had referred
to 'your mother' suggested they were only half-brothers.

Robyn envied the feeling and understanding that
flowed so effortlessly between the two men. She
wished...but too many years had separated her from
her two older sisters. They had been close to each other,
not to her.

Her life might have been a whole lot different if she
had had an older brother who would have stood by her.
Someone that she could always count on...

'Well, I've signed you in and got your room-key. Let's
collect your luggage,' Davey said matter-of-factly.

He turned his brother back towards Robyn and smiled at her. Really smiled. The effect was brilliant. Yet Robyn could not overcome the sense of unease that it wasn't quite genuine...that the smile was thought out...planned...like his last comment to her...precisely calculated!

'You didn't introduce me properly to your companion, Julian. There's a stirring in my blood that tells me it's somehow fateful,' he declared with an amusement that didn't quite overshadow the note of seriousness behind it.

'Miss Robyn Walker, my brother, David Lassiter,' Julian supplied somewhat tersely.

'How long are you here for, Robyn?' asked David, dropping all formality as he took her hand.

'A week,' she answered, aware of his brother's impatient frown and deliberately ignoring it. Julian Lassiter had a lot to learn about civility.

'It's a fine place,' David enthused. 'You can't fail to enjoy yourself.'

'I'm sure I shall.'

Her suitcase had been placed on the same trolley as Julian's, and the bellhop started wheeling it away. 'Registration inside, ma'am,' he called as he noticed her enquiring look.

'Sorry if I embarrassed you,' David said.

'Not at all,' Robyn replied lightly.

'I should have known that Julian wouldn't...I guess it was hope for the future.' He threw the remark at his brother as they all three followed the bellhop.

Julian sliced him a quelling look.

A *perpetual* widower... Robyn wondered if he had children. Not that it was any of her business. Hadn't she decided that she wanted nothing more to do with Julian Lassiter?

'I hope you enjoy your holiday, Miss Walker,' he said politely as they entered the lobby. Again his tone was dismissive.

'Thank you.' She flicked him a frigid smile. 'And thank you once again for your kindness. I hope you both enjoy your stay here also,' she added with a little more warmth directed at David.

And on that note she parted from them, going her independent way to the registration desk, denying herself any further interest in either of the Lassiter brothers.

But she felt eyes boring into her back.

She could not resist the need to look over her shoulder...just a quick glance. To see who it was.

But it was only David Lassiter's gaze that had followed her, not Julian's. And yet, the intentness, the directness of that look was unnerving. It was so assessing, so purposeful, so intimate, that for the third time today Robyn felt herself involved in an encounter which carried a deeper dimension than she had ever experienced before in her life.

CHAPTER THREE

ROBYN worked hard at enjoying herself. And she had every encouragement to do so. Everything about the hotel was fabulous, exotic, undoubtedly unique. Robyn marvelled at the genius that had combined and harmonised so much of what was beautiful in nature with the artistry of man. There was no doubt in her mind now that everything she had heard about the Hyatt-Regency on Maui was true. It was a masterpiece of human imagination.

The only problem was, she wished she had someone with her to share the pleasures. Julian Lassiter had hit on one truth that she could not deny.

She had spent the last few hours of the afternoon wandering through the grounds, marvelling at the landscaping of the eighteen acres on which the hotel stood. The path she had taken led under the twisted branches of tropical trees which spread over massed ferns and exotic plants: bush orchids and lilies and flowers she had never seen before.

She had come across several honeymoon couples—at least they looked as if they were—pointing things out to each other, smiling happily...lovingly. Robyn had passed them by quickly, not wanting to be reminded of Larry, and what she didn't have.

The first section of the pool she came to was like a natural formation in a primitive setting: a waterfall spilling over rocks, a suspension bridge of rope and wood planking, swinging precariously across it, and the

brilliant spill of bougainvillaea trailing to the water's
edge. Beyond a grotto of rocks, the pool was extended
among spongy green lawns and graceful palm trees, and,
still further, the fascination of a Japanese garden with
its dwarfed trees and shrubs.

Everywhere the landscape was enhanced with artefacts
from China, Bali, New Guinea, Japan, Thailand: sculp-
tures of deities, Buddhas, elephants, deer, camels—surprising and delighting the eye in unexpected places. And
then there were the birds: flamingoes and peacocks
strutting over the lawns, and other exotic species twit-
tering through the trees.

But she didn't see Julian Lassiter or his brother. Not
that she really wanted anything further to do with them,
Robyn argued to herself. It was just that seeing them
might have made her feel less alone in such a crowd of
strangers. After all, they were Australian like herself.

And she couldn't help feeling curious about them.
Why was Julian Lassiter a *perpetual* widower? Why
didn't he like women? Was it something to do with the
woman he had married, or had something happened—
like the near-accident this afternoon—and a woman who
could have rescued someone hadn't done so?

Whatever the reason, it certainly hadn't impaired his
sexuality. She wondered if he hated the need that had
simmered in his eyes when he had first looked at her.
He had denied it in the taxi, said that he didn't have the
time, the need, or the inclination...and he had proved
his point with cutting emphasis.

Although, to be completely fair, he probably did have
other things on his mind. Like worrying about his
brother. David Lassiter was not a well man. That had
been obvious even before his angry comment—'It's my

life . . . what's left of it.' And why had he looked at her in such a searching, assessing way?

Robyn tried to shrug off the thoughts. She had enough problems of her own without concerning herself with the Lassiters'. And she wasn't going to get depressed by dwelling on them, either. She was here to enjoy herself!

It was early evening now, and Robyn paused again in the hotel's central court, savouring its unique ambience. It was open to the sky, surrounded by some eight or so storeys of accommodation, but dominated by the huge banyan tree whose spreading limbs had been cut to fit the extraordinary architecture. Palm trees stretched upwards from mounded lawns and lush gardens. Brass hoops on stands with feeder dishes tempted parrots to roost, their brilliant plumage adding more exotica to the scene.

Very casually she scanned the groups of hotel guests who were enjoying pre-dinner cocktails in the Weeping Banyan bar. The pleasant lounge area was set to one side of the central atrium and overlooked the grounds below. Most of the cane armchairs were occupied, but not by Julian and David Lassiter.

Annoyed with herself for even looking for them, Robyn pushed her feet on towards Lahaina corridor which led to the restaurant where she wanted to dine. She paused to drink in the magnificence of the seven-foot-high, blue-on-white porcelain Chinese vase which graced the last garden in the atrium. This was what she had come for. To take pleasure in all there was to see and do.

Guarding the corridor were two bronze lions from Thailand. Robyn smiled at their fierce expressions and passed on by the boutiques that catered for the guests' convenience and pleasure. Maybe she would look through them tomorrow, or the next day, Robyn thought idly as she eyed their luxury wares, but she didn't really intend to buy anything except a memento or two.

She reached the staircase which led down to the premier restaurant in the hotel, Swan Court, and paused to admire the huge chandelier overhead—tiers and tiers of glass shells lit by an amber light. She loved everything about the hotel, and her heart lifted with even more anticipation as she walked down to the half-way landing that overlooked the dining-area below.

The room was shaped in a series of hexagons; its outer walls—at least twenty feet high—were open to an artificial lake where several swans swam up and down with stately grace. A piano was being played with rippling smoothness. The tables were dressed in white linen cloths and elegant dinnerware, subdued candle-lights flickering in glass cylinders. Robyn was pleased to see that several tables were vacant. She hadn't thought to book ahead.

She had dressed simply in a white sundress and high-heeled white sandals, thinking if she was turned away from Swan Court she could just as easily go to one of the other restaurants and not look too out of place. But she really fancied trying out the best on this, her first night here. However, her expectation was very quickly dashed on her arrival at the reception desk when she confessed she didn't have a reservation.

'I'm sorry. All the tables are already booked. You could try Spats. It's very good. Or failing that, the Lahaina Provision Company or the Pavilion,' the hostess told her, listing all the restaurants that were now open.

'Thank you,' Robyn murmured, disappointed, but resolving to have a little more foresight tomorrow.

She was still drinking in the unique features of the room as she turned to leave, and inadvertently collided with someone just arriving. 'Oh! I beg your...' Her voice faltered, her mind jumbling into incoherent shock as her eyes lifted to Julian Lassiter's unmistakable face. Inscrutable hazel eyes caught her gaze and held it.

'Good evening, Miss Walker,' he said coolly.

She jerked back as if she had been bitten by the accidental contact. 'Mr Lassiter...' She nodded stiffly. If she had to bump into someone, why did it have to be him? *Him*, with his frosty, imperturbable dignity! It made her feel such an awkward fool.

She recollected herself with some difficulty. 'Please excuse me...'

'Have you dined already?'

It was David Lassiter who spoke. She hadn't even noticed him standing next to his brother until he drew her attention with his question.

'No. I didn't think to make a reservation and all the tables are booked. I was going somewhere else,' Robyn explained quickly, the words tripping out automatically as she fought down her squirming self-consciousness.

She might have been looking for the Lassiters—out of idle curiosity—but seeing them from a detached distance was one thing. Actually confronting them like this was horribly disconcerting.

'Oh, I'm sure they could fit an extra chair at our table.' David raised an eyebrow at the hostess behind Robyn. 'That can be done, can't it?' he said with persuasive charm.

'Certainly, Mr Lassiter,' was the prompt answer, coated with indulgence for a favoured customer.

'No... please,' Robyn protested. Faced with the immediate proposition, the thought of furthering any acquaintance with these two disturbing men stirred a tense apprehension. 'I don't want to intrude,' she said firmly.

David smiled at her. 'Nonsense! This is where you wanted to be, and it will be our pleasure to have your company. At least, I shall enjoy it...' he flashed a hard look at his brother '...and Julian will have to put up with it.'

Robyn sought desperately to decline the invitation with some tactful retreat. 'Thank you, but...'

'The matter is settled, Miss Walker,' Julian interrupted with autocratic command. 'It will be our pleasure to entertain you.'

He had changed into a green silk shirt and fawn trousers, but had lost no physical impact in the process. The more casual attire lent a heart-thumping dimension of sex-appeal to his strong masculinity. A tremor of fear wrenched Robyn's stomach. She did not want to feel attracted to him in any way. He was trouble. She had no doubt about that now.

And she couldn't believe that he would want her with his brother, that he could possibly mean what he said. She searched her mind for a polite way of saying no.

'This way, Mr Lassiter,' the hostess urged in the background.

David took Robyn's arm, turning her to accompany him. 'Australians have to stick together on foreign soil,' he said gravely, but his manner exuded a quiet friendliness that put Robyn further off balance.

Julian stepped forward on her other side, effectively imprisoning her between them. 'The food here is very good,' he said, again taking her acceptance for granted. 'You'll enjoy it.'

She was trapped by the situation. Short of making a scene and bringing unwanted attention to herself, Robyn could not see how to escape from the Lassiters.

And why should she? came the rebellious thought. She didn't really want to spend the evening alone, eating by herself, watching everyone around her with partners or friends. Even if David Lassiter only wanted to use her as a diversion, and Julian Lassiter didn't want her at all, they could both serve as a diversion for her.

Besides, she had wanted to try this restaurant tonight, and now she had the opportunity to do so. And the opportunity to settle some of her curiosity about the Lassiters. It could be quite interesting...challenging...satisfying. She had learnt how to handle herself in any man's company, and she was not about to let David or Julian Lassiter upset her unduly. She knew what to expect from them, and she would not let it happen.

CHAPTER FOUR

THEY were led to one of the best waterside tables—naturally, Robyn thought cynically—but her cynicism didn't warp her pleasure in being seated exactly where she would have wished. It was unfortunate, however, that David chose to sit on her right, putting Julian directly opposite her. She would have found it easier to ignore him if the seating had been the other way around.

A young and handsome waiter in a silver-grey suit introduced himself and enquired about pre-dinner cocktails. Robyn declined, content to sip the glass of iced water that was provided at every table. David asked for the wine-list.

Rather than look at either brother, Robyn's gaze travelled around the room, noting the hexagonal mirrors in the ceiling, the two stands of flowerbeds in the same shape—massed with vivid blooms, the windows at the far end carved with white feathers. Only two wide stone steps separated her from the water's edge and, as she turned to the sound of the water which cascaded over tumbled rocks on one side of the lake, two black swans sailed right up to the steps beside her.

'They were imported from Western Australia,' David remarked, 'but don't ask me where the white swans come from. I don't know.'

As she turned to him, he handed her the wine-list, inviting her to look through it. Even the least expensive wines were beyond her budget. Although she made a good living out of her business—after struggling hard

to establish a reliable reputation with the tour agencies—
making money was not so easy that she could ever bring
herself to spend it in a profligate fashion. Only for a
good bottle of champagne for a very special occasion
would she ever pay over twenty dollars for a bottle.

She shook her head in bemusement as she noticed a
Lafite '61 at fifteen hundred dollars and a '45 Mouton-
Rothschild at twenty-four hundred dollars. She won-
dered if anyone ever actually ordered them.

'Nothing that strikes your fancy?' David asked as she
handed it back to him.

She smiled. 'I'm riding on a high with the beauty of
this place. I don't need anything more.'

But she didn't stint herself when it came to the menu.
Swan Court was a Travel Holiday award-winning restaurant and Robyn loved good food. She ordered a
starter of smoked salmon and sturgeon, then duckling
with a honey and macadamia sauce as the main course.

' . . . and the Lafite '61,' Julian said coolly as he completed his order.

Robyn stared at him in pure shock. How could he
throw so much money away on a bottle of wine? For
her it was three weeks' work just to make that amount
of money.

'There's a '45 Mouton on the list, but it might be a
bit over the hill,' he said to David. 'And I want you to
have the best.'

His brother nodded. 'Always a risk with old wines.'

They thought nothing of it, Robyn realised with a sense
of awe. They were used to having what they wanted,
regardless of the cost. She had instinctively known that
Julian Lassiter would demand and take everything first-
class for granted, but this degree of wealth was almost

beyond Robyn's comprehension. It seemed ... immoral, somehow ... almost obscene.

The hazel-green eyes suddenly locked on to hers, and Robyn had the disagreeable feeling that Julian Lassiter sensed her inner disapproval. His thin smile held a mocking twist. 'Not drinking ... don't smoke ... what vices do you have, Miss Walker? I'm sure Davey and I would both like to know.'

She deliberately held his gaze in challenge, denying the nervous flutter in her heart. No way was she going to let him control this encounter! Or intimidate her! 'Some people have called me a workaholic,' she said with a dismissive shrug.

'Oh? What do you do?' The caustic way the question was asked seemed to imply that, whatever she did, it wouldn't be worthy of note.

'I'd prefer not to bore you with it, Mr Lassiter,' she retorted sweetly. 'I'm sure ...'

'I'd like to know,' David interrupted.

Robyn turned towards the brother, and the speculative interest in his eyes suggested that he would give her a fair hearing. A prickle of pride urged her to answer him, and enthusiasm crept into her voice as she started to explain how she put together tour packages at the wholesale level, which she then marketed to the travel industry.

It was a side of tourism that the two men had never seen, and as Robyn outlined how she would get an idea or concept and develop it into a travel theme, she sensed that Julian's interest was captured, as well as David's, although the older man kept up his mask of reserve. He disdained any questions, but his brother asked what tours she had put together recently.

'Ireland...land of saints and scholars; the pre-Columbian civilisations of the Mayas, Incas and Aztecs; the old culture of Russia; the new China; Ancient Egypt...' She grinned. 'And to have something on home ground, the wonders of the Great Barrier Reef.'

'You know so much about history and the different cultures of the world,' David commented, and Robyn thought she detected a note of admiration.

'You learn,' she said drily, thinking of the hours she pored over books in the State library. But they were good hours. She enjoyed broadening her knowledge and picking up little-known facts.

David praised her initiative and flair, and although Robyn felt pleased with his compliments she could not shake off the uncomfortable impression that he was making judgements about her in some way. His eyes were too sharply intelligent—probing, weighing, analysing.

'You went straight into work after school,' he said after some consideration. 'You didn't consider going on to tertiary education...university?'

'Perhaps Miss Walker didn't have the necessary qualifications, Davey,' Julian Lassiter put in with dry amusement.

It was the first comment he had made since she had begun to talk of her work, and the suggested slight on her intelligence had Robyn's chin lifting in aggressive pride. Her blue eyes stabbed resentment at him. She was not going to let him put her down again.

'It so happens I was dux of my school, Mr Lassiter.'

She didn't give him the explanation that it had been much easier to stay in her room studying than to suffer the company of her second stepfather. That was nobody's business but her own.

'I preferred to make my own living as soon as possible,' she added, with a slight echo of the determination that had driven her to get out from under the roof of her mother's third husband at the earliest possible moment.

'You would have gone into the arts field, anyway,' David remarked, 'and I doubt that you would have learnt anything more useful than you've learnt yourself. I like the way your mind works,' he added with a nod of satisfaction.

Robyn wasn't sure she wanted or even liked David Lassiter's stamp of approval. Somehow it smacked of condescension—you've measured up, so now you can be admitted to the charmed circle. However, it was satisfying to have proved to these Lassiters that she was as good as anyone else.

Their first course arrived at the table and, with the secret pleasure of having knocked some of the superiority out of Julian Lassiter, Robyn attacked the salmon and sturgeon with good appetite.

'So you're a career-woman,' Julian remarked as he polished off his dish of *escargots*.

'Very much so,' Robyn replied emphatically. Particularly after her all-too-recent disillusionment with Larry!

'No intention of ever getting married?' he mocked.

Again her eyes locked on to his, and an electric charge of antagonism crackled between them. 'None whatsoever,' Robyn drawled.

'Why is that?' David asked curiously.

She tore her eyes away from the hard scepticism in Julian Lassiter's and turned to his brother with a careless shrug. 'My mother has had three husbands so far. My two older sisters are each on their second marriages. I prefer not to mess up my life...and others'...by taking emotional decisions that don't work out. I'll make it on my own.'

David nodded in approval, as if she had just passed another examination with flying colours. 'What about children? You don't mind the thought of going through life without ever being a mother?' he asked.

'Bearing a child would spoil her figure,' Julian observed sardonically.

David frowned at him. 'Don't apply the obsession your wife had about her body to every other woman, Julian. That's not fair. If Robyn decides not to have a baby, it won't be for that reason.'

But the hazel-green eyes kept taunting Robyn. 'Let the lady answer,' he challenged with silky softness.

His wife! Of course, she would have to have been beautiful...no second-best for Julian Lassiter! And yet, there had been hurt and pain behind that statement. His wife had not been altogether perfect, since she had obviously refused to give him children. And for some obscure reason Robyn was glad about that.

'I would like to have a child of my own,' she answered truthfully. 'And one day, when I feel financially secure, and the business can run for some time without me, I might just do that, Mr Lassiter.'

And she might, too. Why not? Other women did it. And she would love to have a child. It was one of the reasons why she had accepted Larry's proposal.

'Without benefit of marriage?' Julian Lassiter prodded.

Her eyes hardened. 'I'm not of the opinion that two parents are necessarily better than one. At least my child would have all the love and attention that I can give it. Above all else, he or she would know it was wanted...and loved with all my heart.'

And there would be no men messing them around, she added in silent and savage bitterness.

'Perhaps that's not a healthy attitude. Smothering instead of mothering. Spare the rod, spoil the child,' came the sceptical rejoinder.

'It's healthier than a lot of others,' she flared back at him, recalling her own upbringing so vividly that all the old hurts pulsed through her heart. And somehow Julian Lassiter was bound up with all those men who should have been something other than what they were. Why was he so intent on wounding her, on putting her down?

'You had an unhappy childhood, Robyn?' David enquired.

She was wound up so tight that she had forgotten where she was; completely lost to the beauty and elegance of her surroundings; her whole being channelled into the tense battle being waged between herself and the man on the other side of the table.

She dragged herself out of it, made a conscious effort to relax, sat back in her chair and determined to get the conversation off herself. 'I coped,' she answered briefly. 'How about you?'

David seemed lost in another world. He answered her slowly, with a faint smile. 'Oh, I was spoilt rotten. Being the only child of a late marriage, I had parents who were old enough to spend their time doting on me, and a ready-made big brother who smoothed the path for me to do whatever I wanted to do. Couldn't have been more perfect.'

'And what do you do?' she asked.

The smile faded and was replaced by a look of quiet intensity. 'I'm involved in scientific research.'

Robyn was about to ask him to be more specific when Julian cut in. 'Davey has been nominated for a Nobel Prize because of his work on the viral causes of cancer,' he stated quietly, but Robyn could sense the pride behind his words.

'Julian is always making out I'm important,' David said in sharp demur.

'You are,' Julian insisted, and the atmosphere was suddenly choked with deep and intense emotion. 'If we could change places...'

'Don't go on! I know!' David almost snapped at him. His whiter-than-white skin was stretched tightly over his face. 'What you do is important too, Julian,' he said in a softer, appeasing tone.

It was clear that David didn't want his work discussed. And, by the look of him, Robyn wondered if his work might not have a personal motive. He certainly did not have the appearance of a well man, despite his apparent appetite for good food and wine. She instinctively responded to his need to shift the focus of attention away from himself.

'And what do you do, Mr Lassiter?' she asked Julian, who had withdrawn behind his austere mask of control.

'He makes the money that allows a lot of basic research to be done,' David said.

Julian threw him an ironic smile. 'Nice to have some useful function.'

And this time Robyn was instantly aware of the disillusionment behind his hard cynicism. Did he want to wound because he was so wounded himself? But it was not her fault, she reasoned angrily.

David relaxed, turning back to Robyn with a twinkle of amusement enlivening his light green eyes. 'Julian doesn't realise how important he is to me. He heads the

Lassiter Corporation, which manufactures pharmaceutical drugs and all sorts of medical equipment for doctors and hospitals. He took over the chairmanship from our father, and has run it so successfully that I could do as I pleased. And that was what I wanted.'

So her surmise had been right this afternoon, Robyn thought with satisfaction. Julian Lassiter would know all the chairmen of the boards.

The waiter arrived to serve them their main courses and the conversation dropped to a few appreciative comments on the meal. The wine was poured with great deference. David offered Robyn a glass but she refused it categorically. It would be like drinking gold, she thought with a slight shudder. Only people like the Lassiters could feel comfortable about that. The two men quietly enthused over its fine quality.

Robyn's duckling was beautifully tender, the honey and macadamia sauce a little sweet for her taste but interestingly different from the more traditional cherry or orange sauce that accompanied the dish. She was halfway through her meal when David Lassiter suddenly put down his utensils and clenched his hands.

'Davey?' The enquiry from Julian was sharp and tense.

'Sorry, I'll have to leave you,' he said, a ghastly look on his face. 'It's the Methotrexate I'm taking. I've got some Pyridoxine in my room to settle the nausea down.'

He climbed unsteadily to his feet. Julian was instantly beside him, gripping his arm.

'No. I can make it on my own,' David insisted, his strong face set in proud independence. 'I want you to stay here and finish the meal. And don't waste the wine. It's a good bottle.'

He turned to Robyn. 'I'm so sorry I have to leave you like this. You've put an idea in my mind, and I wanted to ask you about it. But it will have to wait until later.'

He left, taking quick, jerky strides away from them. Julian remained standing, his gaze concentrated on his brother until David moved out of sight. Then he sank back on to his chair, his vexation at having to stay with Robyn unstated but very apparent. He glared at her as if it were all her fault.

She refused to be defensive about something she hadn't done. 'You can leave me here any time you want,' she said bluntly. 'I hadn't expected to have company, anyway.'

'Quite the self-contained person, aren't you?' he commented cuttingly. 'Do go on with your meal. I'm sure nothing could spoil it for you.' He picked up his wine-glass and drained its contents as if it were water.

'Thank you, but I've had enough.' In truth, her appetite had deserted her. 'He's very ill, isn't he?' she observed quietly.

Sheer naked rage looked back at her; a rage wrapped in frustration that there was nothing he could do about it no matter how much power and wealth he had at his fingertips. 'Yes. He's dying. He has three months...possibly six months left to live. Does that satisfy your curiosity?'

'I'm so sorry,' Robyn whispered, shocked and shaken by the dreadful finality of those words.

'We all are,' Julian muttered bitterly. 'It was all so unnecessary!'

'Please explain,' she asked softly, virtually inviting him to vent more of his bottled-up anger on her. He was hurting very badly, and, while he had given her no reason to feel any sympathy for him, some well of compassion in her heart prompted her to ease his pain if she could.

Julian Lassiter might not care about himself or anything else, but he loved his brother—with the kind of love Robyn had never known. Her mother and sisters had always been wrapped up in their own lives, and Larry... his need for her had only been sexual. Not one of them would have wanted to change places with her if she were struck down with a terminal illness. To love so deeply... was she herself capable of it?

All these years, protecting herself from hurt... keeping herself to herself... expecting little and giving little... and the truth of it was, she hadn't really loved Larry, not to the depth where he was indispensable to her. Not like Julian loved his brother.

He had sunk into a dark brooding at her soft offer of a sympathetic ear for his pain. 'I'd like to know,' she said, wanting to reach out to him.

He suddenly shot her a resentful look, then spoke with a weary disgust in his voice. 'Davey was working with heavy cobalt isotopes to mark molecules in lethal viruses. There was a laboratory accident, and he was infected. He is now suffering from acute leukaemia.'

He sighed and leaned back in his chair, surveying her through hooded eyes. 'Hardly the topic for the first night of your vacation. Davey won't thank me for telling you, but I'm sure you can keep it to yourself.'

'I'm not completely without perception, Mr Lassiter. Your brother doesn't want pity.'

'No. He's like you, Miss Walker. He doesn't want emotions messing up... what's left of his life. Perhaps you're both right. Who knows?' His mouth twisted into a grimace of personal repugnance. 'He's offered himself as a human guinea pig in order to find out whether it's the virus or the heavy isotopes that are causing the pro-liferation of the leukocytes.'

Robyn's heart squeezed at the thought of how his mother and Julian would feel about seeing him suffer unnecessarily, but she could not help but admire David Lassiter's fortitude for the sake of knowledge that might help others.

'Is he married?' she asked, wanting to stop Julian from sinking into morose thoughts.

'No wife...no children...just medical research. That's his legacy to the world, Miss Walker.' He sighed more heavily and shook his head. 'At least it's some satis-faction to him.'

Robyn nodded. 'What are you doing here?'

'Davey wanted...a last taste of all that was most pleasurable in this world...before things got too grim for him to enjoy them.'

A lump formed in Robyn's throat, choking any thought of continuing the conversation. She felt ashamed of having been critical about the extravagant choice of wine.

The hazel-green eyes suddenly stabbed across the table in a hard personal rejection of her sympathy, her presence, everything about her. 'So you see, Miss Walker, I'm prepared to agree to any of my brother's wishes, regardless of my own,' he said very pointedly.

The brush with tragedy made fighting with Julian Lassiter a distasteful exercise. She had done nothing to deserve his rudeness, but she held her tongue. This was neither the time or the place to say anything.

Their waiter came by, refilled the empty wineglass and removed the dinner-plates. 'Coffee?'

'Yes, please,' Robyn answered.

'Sir?'

'No, thank you.'

The waiter started to tell them about the sweets which were set out in smorgasbord fashion near the reception desk, but both of them quickly rejected any continuation of the meal.

Silence fell. Julian Lassiter obviously had no inclination to break it and Robyn sat wondering why on earth she felt...involved...with the man. Even when he seemed totally withdrawn, she could not completely withdraw herself and ignore him.

The bill was presented with the coffee—only one bill and placed at Julian Lassiter's hand. 'I'm afraid you've made a mistake,' Robyn said quickly, holding the waiter with a commanding look. 'My meal was separate from the gentlemen's. I need a separate bill.'

Julian Lassiter flicked her a sharp look as he leaned forward and picked up the pen to sign the account. 'You are our guest, Miss Walker.'

'I accepted a chair, not a meal, Mr Lassiter,' she retorted determinedly. Compassion was one thing, her pride was quite another. And she would not be beholden to him for anything after the way he had treated her. 'I do not wish to accept any charity from you.' She lifted her gaze to the waiter's. 'Please take that back and separate the accounts.'

He hesitated, then, as Julian Lassiter sat back with the form unsigned, the waiter decided to do Robyn's bidding. 'Sorry, ma'am. My mistake,' he murmured, picking up the plate and hurrying off.

'Charity, Miss Walker?' There was a dry note of amusement in the question.

She gave it to him straight between the eyes. 'You bundled me into your taxi, Mr Lassiter. Both you and your brother combined to bundle me to this table. You arrogantly assume that your decision is the ultimate word. I let you get away with it twice before because it suited me, but not this time. It didn't cost you any more to allow me to share your taxi, but this is different and I don't want to take your money.'

He actually laughed—at least, a short harsh sound that approximated to laughter. 'You do surprise me, Miss Walker.'

Incensed by his amusement when she had meant to put him down, Robyn raised a mocking eyebrow. 'How diverting for you, Mr Lassiter. I'm afraid you don't surprise me at all.'

Then, on second reflection, she added, 'No, I take that back. You certainly did surprise me with your offer this afternoon. It wasn't in character.'

Antagonism vibrated across the table. 'What would you know of my character?' he queried softly.

Quite a lot, Robyn thought, but she was not about to give him the satisfaction of trying to score any more points off her. 'I'm not prepared to say. I'm sure you approve of that answer.'

His eyes narrowed.

Robyn tossed caution and politeness aside. 'For some reason, you don't like me, Mr Lassiter,' she said bluntly. 'Maybe it's the very same reason I don't like you. There's something about you that I find very unsettling. I suspect that's why you treat me as you do.'

His mouth thinned and curved slightly to one side. 'That's very perceptive,' he said slowly.

They sat staring at each other, neither prepared to give an inch, yet bound by something that would not release them.

'Then I think we should try to avoid each other,' Robyn suggested, a proud disdain creeping into her voice. 'Do you agree?'

'Yes.' The word was almost a hiss through his clenched teeth.

The waiter returned with separate bills, apologising again for the error. As if a truce had been called, they both leaned forward and signed for their meals.

Robyn picked up her handbag and rose to her feet. Julian Lassiter towered beside her. Knowing that he would accompany her up the stairs, Robyn said nothing. She led off through the dining-room, intensely aware of his following her. She refused to make any acknowledgement of his presence as she started up the wide staircase. He remained one step behind her. She gave him time to reach the Lahaina corridor, then turned to face him. She did not offer her hand.

'Goodnight, Mr Lassiter,' she said coolly, her eyes meeting his with a blandness she was far from feeling. 'And goodbye.'

'Goodnight, Miss Walker.' His mouth quirked. 'And may I say you walk very well.'

'I can also stand and fight. I hope you remember that, Mr Lassiter.'

'Goodbye,' he grated, annoyed at having given her the opening for a return strike at him.

She swung on her heel and walked away, conscious of eyes boring after her, but she didn't glance back this time. She knew more about him now . . . knew his power to probe and wound . . . knew he was very, very dangerous to her peace of mind.

CHAPTER FIVE

ROBYN'S room was on the ground floor of the Napili wing. She had no doubt that the Lassiters would have Regency Club rooms or suites—the ultimate in exclusiveness at this hotel—so she knew Julian would not follow her beyond the central courtyard where that section of the accommodation had its own set of lifts. But, after his taunting little comment that she walked well, Robyn was uncomfortably conscious of her whole body.

She could not relax until she was safely enclosed in the privacy of a lift in the Napili wing, and all she could think of was getting to her room and locking the rest of the world out. More specifically, that part of the world inhabited by Julian Lassiter.

And his brother.

She felt sorry for David Lassiter, but she didn't want to think about him. She didn't want to meet him again, either. It was bad enough having been touched by the tragedy of his illness tonight. She was supposed to be relaxing, having a good time, enjoying the fruits of her labours, forgetting about Larry. That was why she had come here, not to get involved in something that hurt.

And there was nothing she could do for him. It wasn't really selfish of her to block him out of her life. He wouldn't want her to moon over his situation. David Lassiter was a man who could make hard choices and stick to them, even against his family's wishes. And he had his brother with him.

Robyn now understood Julian's tension in the taxi this afternoon: gearing himself to keep his emotions under control, to do and be whatever Davey wanted for whatever precious time remained, to support without ever letting his own inner pain be intrusive or oppressive, to savour moments of closeness and store up lasting memories...

Tears blurred Robyn's eyes as she jammed her door-key in the lock. She dashed them away with the back of her hand, impatient with her sentimentality. Forget the Lassiters, she told herself severely, and tried to slam the door after her as she entered the room, but the air-lock prevented even that outlet for her emotions.

It was a terrace room, as spacious and as well appointed as those in the more expensive sections of the hotel, but with a limited view of the grounds. Robyn didn't mind that at all. She did not intend to spend much time in her room, apart from sleeping.

She paused at the walk-in wardrobe section and took off her high-heels. Then, to put a more decisive end to this disturbing evening, she stripped off her dress, hung it up, walked over to the vanity-table and washed off her make-up. The hotel provided a *yukata*, a long cotton Japanese lounging robe, and Robyn slipped on the comfortable garment as she walked the length of her bed-sitting-room to the glass double doors which opened on to her balcony.

The air outside was warm and balmy, with a light breeze wafting in from the sea. The thick growth of the tropical garden seemed magically primitive in the dim glow of path-lights. Robyn could hear dance music being played somewhere down near the pool area, and remembered that the hotel activities programme had listed dancing under the stars.

She leaned on the balcony railing and closed her eyes, letting the music drift around her.

Dancing...not in a stuffy little nightclub with amplifiers blasting out a migraine beat and everyone performing their cleverest aerobics...that was fine for working off some energy, but it wasn't the stuff that dreams were made of. And, however practical and down to earth she was in real life, Robyn secretly yearned for the love and romance that never quite came her way. Not even with Larry.

Like the romance of dancing under the stars, with the roll of the ocean in the background...two people holding each other, cheek brushing cheek, moving together with sensuous grace, her fingers curling into the thickness of his black hair, his hand caressing the bare skin of her back...

Robyn shivered, then jolted upright as she realised that the man she had been picturing was Julian Lassiter. She was becoming positively neurotic about that wretched man, and it had to stop. It couldn't lead to anything good. And yet...she could not help wondering what it would be like to be held in his arms...touched... kissed...caressed...loved by him.

She remembered how she had frozen up at any kind of petting those first few years after getting away from her second stepfather. Then for a while she had suffered a certain number of physical liberties from the men she dated, to see if it really was pleasurable, not liking the thought that she was unnatural and missing out on things she should enjoy. But it hadn't really worked for her, not as it was supposed to.

Even with Larry.

He had been quite intrigued to find her still a virgin at twenty-six. With patience and persistence he had set about breaking down her inhibitions, and she had not wanted to lose him. They had a lot of common interests and she had enjoyed her relationship with him more than any other she had ever had.

He had excited her enough to make her willing to advance their relationship to a sexual one. After all, if they were going to be married, she had to go to bed with him sooner or later, and she wanted to please him. Wanted to know what it was like to love in the full physical sense.

And it was all right. Not exactly the wild, wonderful thing one read about, but maybe she had a low sex-drive—whatever that meant. Larry had seemed satisfied. But after they had gone to bed together Larry had changed. He hadn't wanted her so much any more. In the end, he hadn't wanted her at all.

A wash of misery darkened Robyn's thoughts. Obviously she had been the wrong woman for Larry. Perhaps he had been the wrong man for her. She wanted to feel what she was supposed to feel...

The telephone in her room buzzed.

Robyn frowned. Who could be ringing her? She glanced at her watch...almost eleven o'clock. Of course her mother and sisters knew where she was, but only in the direst emergency would they call from Sydney.

She stepped back into her room and slid the door shut behind her. With a quick yank she pulled the curtains across to ensure privacy before striding to the bedside-table where the telephone kept buzzing its summons. She snatched it up, her heart thumping in alarm.

'Hello, Robyn Walker.'

'Miss Walker, Robyn...'

She could hardly believe her ears. Julian Lassiter's voice? Or was it David's?

'Who's speaking please?' she snapped into the pause that followed her name.

'Julian Lassiter. I hope you weren't asleep.'

Him? Calling her Robyn? Had he been thinking of her along the same lines as she had just been thinking of him...fantasising what she might be like...? An awful squirming heat flooded through Robyn's body. Of course not, her mind screamed at her. He didn't have the time, the need, or the inclination. And he didn't even like her!

'No, I wasn't asleep,' she replied as coolly as she could. 'What do you want, Mr Lassiter?'

He sighed. 'I apologise for calling at such a late hour. I know it must seem unreasonable to you, but I want...I have to see you, talk to you...now...if you would be so kind.'

The strained note in his voice; the difficulty he obviously had in bringing himself to ask the favour; the fact that he was virtually begging her—all intrigued Robyn. But pride insisted that she should make him squirm, too. He had given her no reason to like him. And of course she didn't!

'I thought we agreed...'

'Yes, I know,' he cut in quickly. 'But this is...something else. I don't wish to discuss it over the phone. But it could be to your advantage. Please, could we meet somewhere? I assure you it is important, and possibly in your own interests to hear me out.'

And what could he mean by that? Robyn wondered. As far as she was concerned, her interests were best served by avoiding him like the plague. But he had stirred her curiosity to the point where she couldn't resist hearing what he had to say.

'Robyn?' Anxious—anxious enough to drop the distance of formality!

Well, she wasn't going to drop her distance. Not after the way he had treated her. 'I'm not dressed, Mr Lassiter, and I...'

'If it suits your convenience better, I'll come down to your room,' he said quickly.

Robyn had been about to ask for a little time to get dressed, but on second thoughts she decided it was probably best to meet him on her own territory. It would put him even more on his mettle to behave well towards her, and she could keep the whole distance of the room between them while she heard what he had to say.

'Very well, Mr Lassiter. My room in ten minutes.'

'Thank you.' The call was disconnected before she could change her mind.

It was madness to invite any further involvement with Julian Lassiter, Robyn told herself. Yet she could not deny a singing sense of anticipation that lifted her heart and sharpened her mind as she threw off the *yukata*, pulled on a pair of blue slacks and selected the white crocheted top to team with it.

She actually had a tube of lipstick in her hand, lifting it to her mouth, when she stopped herself. Looking respectable was one thing, prettying herself up for Julian Lassiter was quite another. She stared at herself in the mirror, confronting the betraying sparkle in her eyes. She hadn't felt quite so sharply alive in a long time... ever, if she was completely honest.

It was the sense of power, Robyn argued. Julian Lassiter was the last person on earth that she had ever expected to come crawling to her for anything, but that was what he was doing, and eating humble pie in the process. Considering his attitude towards her at dinner, the situation was highly diverting, to say the least. Irresistible.

She almost jumped at the knock on her door. She took a moment to compose herself into cool dignity, then moved unhurriedly to the door to admit her unlikely visitor.

'Thank you,' he murmured, barely looking at her as he passed by into the short hallway. He paused, and the tension emanating from him tangled with Robyn's nerves.

'Go on in. Take a seat,' she invited curtly.

Apart from the sofa which was serviced by a coffee-table and a lamp-table, there were two comfortable chairs next to a small dining-table. But he did not sit down. He remained standing at the far end of the room, patently ill at ease, his gaze flicking over the tourist activity pamphlets that were spread across the coffee-table.

'Would you like a drink?' Robyn asked, moving towards the tallboy that housed the television set and the hospitality bar.

'No. No, thank you,' he amended quickly. 'It was good of you to see me.'

'Not at all.' She gave him a dry smile. 'You piqued my curiosity. Please sit down.'

He made an indeterminate gesture that suggested he was waiting for her to do so. Robyn propped herself on the end of her king-size bed and raised an enquiring eyebrow. 'I'm waiting, Mr Lassiter.'

He was still dressed in the same clothes he'd worn at dinner. For one wayward moment, Robyn wondered if he danced well. But dancing certainly wasn't on his mind. His eyes were dark with turbulent emotion.

'You said...at dinner...that you wanted to have a child of your own.'

'Yes,' she agreed, puzzled that he should bring up the subject again.

'Conditional upon financial security,' he continued, like a trial lawyer drawing out the facts.

'Yes,' she bit out, antagonised by his manner.

'You meant what you said?'

'Mr Lassiter, you made your opinion of me quite clear at the time. I see no point in these questions.'

'My opinion doesn't matter,' he said impatiently. 'Did you mean what you said?'

'Yes,' she snapped.

He drew in a deep breath and slowly exhaled it. 'Then I have a proposition for you.'

The words were quietly spoken, yet they thumped into Robyn's heart like a sledge-hammer. He gave her no time to comment, but plunged on, speaking quickly as if he had rehearsed the lines so many times that he didn't have to think about them.

'We're a very wealthy family. You would never want for anything again. We can come to any kind of financial arrangement you like. Tie it all up legally so you'll feel completely secure. If you want to keep on working after the child is born—and before, for that matter—I'll arrange whatever help you require.'

Was he proposing that she have *his* child? Robyn shook her head, unable to believe what she was hearing.

'I know you said you didn't want marriage,' he continued, punching out his points. 'But there's no question of living together. The legality is necessary so that the child has the Lassiter name. You will have full custody, although I hope you'll be generous enough to grant visiting rights to the family.'

Robyn's mind was whirling. A marriage that was not a marriage...to this man? The pain of a cold, calculated, loveless and brief intimacy...to gain the happiness that a child could bring? Was that what the old lady had foreseen this afternoon?

Everything within her recoiled from such a cold-blooded relationship with Julian Lassiter.

And she wouldn't do it! It was the most insulting thing he had done yet, to propose using her body to serve his purpose, and trample over her feelings as if she were nothing! She was so outraged that he should suggest it that she barely heard the conditions he was laying down.

'I doubt you'd find a better man to father your child if you looked for a million years,' he finally concluded.

The sheer blazing arrogance of that statement was the last straw. 'That is a matter of opinion, Mr Lassiter,' she said caustically.

An angry flush suffused his face. 'For God's sake! What more do you want?'

Pride drew her to her feet in haughty disdain of his humiliating proposition. 'I'll tell you what I want, Mr Lassiter. I want to choose for myself.' Her eyes seared him with contempt. 'You came down here thinking you could buy me. And I will not be bought. Not with the great Lassiter name, nor your wealth nor power... nor person,' she finished cuttingly.

A fine film of perspiration broke out on his forehead. His mouth thinned as though he was clenching his teeth. It cost him a great deal of effort to speak quietly and reasonably. 'Of course, the choice is yours. And I'm sorry I offended you. I didn't mean to do that.' His eyes flashed at her, hating the necessity to appease but grimly determined to do it. 'At this stage you must understand my feelings; it's only Davey that counts.'

David? She recalled Julian saying he would do anything for his brother. 'What has David got to do with this?' she asked incredulously.

His chest rose and fell as he fought to retain control of himself. 'I'm sorry if you did not understand. I come here as an intermediary. He felt if he came himself . . . it might pressure you into a false position. He wouldn't do that.'

She stared at him, her mind playing double-loops with all he had said. 'You are not giving me this proposition on your own behalf?' she asked stiltedly.

'No. It would be the last proposition I'd ever make to a woman,' he asserted emphatically.

Not him . . . but David! He wanted her to marry David and bear his child . . . David, who was dying. Robyn could feel the blood draining from her face as shock clenched her heart. She sank back down on the bed. Her mind kept revolving in circles. Not Julian . . . David.

The old lady had been wrong, hopelessly and hideously wrong. All the nervous tension of the last few minutes threatened to dissolve into a wave of hysteria. Robyn grimly fought it down, telling herself she had been stupid ever to have let that prediction stick in her mind. Hadn't she known all along it was nonsense?

But still she shied away from contemplating the reality—the reality of David Lassiter wanting her to bear his child, his name, to continue his lifeline which had such a short time left to run. The pain of it . . . was that what the old lady had seen? Robyn shook her head.

'Please . . .' The word burst from Julian Lassiter, his control breaking at what he saw as a negative response to his proposition. He strode towards her, hands outstretched in desperate appeal. 'Tell me what inducement I can offer that will persuade you! His life is so short. Time is so precious. I can't . . .' His face twisted with anguish. 'I can't go back to him and destroy his one last hope of . . . of leaving something of himself to carry on.'

Then, in the extremity of wrenching despair, he grabbed Robyn's arms and pulled her up, shaking her with the intensity of his need to reach into her and impart his own feeling for his brother. 'You've got to do this! You've got to.'

Tears swam into Robyn's eyes; tears of shock and shame that she had been so slow to comprehend the agony of mind that was now spilling over her.

The fingers bruising her upper arms suddenly relaxed their grip. His hands dropped away. 'I'm sorry,' he rasped. 'I had no right...'

Even through her own blurred vision Robyn saw his eyes shut tight, his face etched in lines of tortured grief for what had to be. His lips moved stiffly as he forced words through them.

'And you have every right...to choose your own path.' His eyes opened a glimmer, raking her pale, shocked face. 'Please, forgive my temerity. I am...not myself. Thank you for your time.'

He moved towards the door, each heavy step burdened with the necessity of returning to his brother with her negative reply. Robyn's heart twisted into a knot of anguish for the man who was waiting, hoping, desperately wanting this one chance at beating the finality of death.

'Julian.' His name croaked from her throat. She swallowed hard. 'Don't go yet.'

He halted, turned slowly, then leaned back against the wall as though he was weary beyond measure. His hooded eyes measured the space back to her. 'You want to draw more blood?' he asked in a resigned taunt.

Robyn held his gaze steadily, ignoring the screaming chaos in her mind and the agitated beat of her heart.

'Why me?' she asked. 'Why would he choose me on such short acquaintance?'

His mouth twisted in dry mockery. 'You won't like the answer.'

'Then that should please you,' she retorted recklessly.

'No. It doesn't please me. There's nothing that can please me at this particular point in time.' He shook his head and pushed himself away from the wall. 'I'm really not in the mood for feeding your ego. Goodbye once again.' He reached for the door-handle.

'I might change my mind.'

He froze.

Robyn herself froze at the enormity of what she had just said.

He turned, very slowly. 'Don't play with me, Robyn.' The words were a bare drift of sound, strained between disbelief and the need to believe.

She didn't know what drove her—compassion, pity?—but the words came to her tongue and were put into speech. 'I'm not playing. I wouldn't play with something that is so... critical ... to another human being. I'm sorry I misunderstood you before. I thought you were talking of yourself. Because your wife hadn't given you a child. I didn't realise you were speaking for David.'

His eyes probed hers with urgent intensity. 'And that makes a difference to you?'

'Perhaps. I ... I don't know.' Her hands twisted together in an agony of uncertainty. How could she commit herself to something that would change her life so irrevocably? Yet her soul writhed at the thought of sending Julian Lassiter away with such a death-dealing blow to his brother.

'I need more time,' she pleaded. 'It's something I would have to think about. The answer is probably no, but I didn't get where I am in business by making snap judgements without considering all the factors. I...I need to know more.'

Her pulse leapt erratically with every step he took in closing the distance between them. His hand lifted, curled around her cheek, lifted her chin. His eyes raked hers, intent on tearing away any veil of deception.

Robyn's chest tightened. She couldn't breathe. His touch on her skin seemed to burn through her brain, scorching away every thought. Her stomach contracted in sheer nervous reaction to his closeness.

'This can't be impulse, Robyn,' he said softly. 'It won't be over in a few moments, as it was with saving the old lady this afternoon. It won't be over in a few days, or even with Davey's death. You will be living with the consequences for the rest of your life. Are you sure you want to know more?'

Fear rippled through her heart, but she couldn't back off. Somehow the gentle touch of his hand and the caring words bound her to him in a sense of sharing that she had never known before. Certainly she had never experienced it in her own family. It gave her a tantalising glimpse of the bond between him and his brother. Would she share that too if she had David's child?

The image of his white hand closing over Julian's shoulder and digging in flashed through her mind, the emotion and understanding so easily imparted and returned. She wanted to say—be like that to me; but the words stuck in her throat.

'Yes,' she whispered. 'I want to know it all.'

His relief was palpable, but his eyes kept probing hers as if he couldn't completely believe in her sincerity. And for a moment there was something else . . . not the sexual speculation of this afternoon, but a deep, ravening need that clawed at her soul and was withdrawn in an instant, short, sharp, finished, its termination underlined by a savage little grimace.

'I started at the wrong place,' he said with a stiff half-smile of apology. 'I thought...' He shook his head. 'Never mind. Let's sit down and begin again.'

He led Robyn to the sofa, saw her seated, drew one of the chairs over to the coffee-table and settled opposite her. Robyn found it difficult to concentrate on what Julian was saying at first. She was too aware of him: his facial expressions; the gestures he made—long, supple fingers; the varying tones of his voice—no longer mocking or cynical, but warm and earnest and caring.

He talked for a long time: stories about Davey's childhood, his schooling, his all-round brilliance—athletics, debating, mathematics, science—his dedication to medical research and the achievements he had made in that field.

'He was always too intensely wrapped up in his work to form anything more than a casual relationship with a woman. He used to say there was time for that when he lost his edge. Most scientists do their best work when they're young, and Davey's only thirty now.'

Julian threw her an anxious look before continuing. 'Davey is an analyst, totally involved in his work. I hope you won't be offended. You have to understand how he thinks. To him it's all a matter of genes.'

He frowned, picking his words with careful tact. 'Physically you're a very fine-looking woman, Robyn. You're also very intelligent. It's not just the ability to achieve academically, it's the way you apply your knowledge, with perception and initiative. He also admires what he calls your sane approach to life.'

Julian drew in a deep breath and met her eyes in an intense plea for understanding. 'Davey sees sex as a means of letting evolution take its own course. For some reason—who can define these impulses?—he saw you and you touched off some...he says an instinctive recognition of possible mateship. Then, at dinner, he was much taken by your abilities...everything about you.'

Assessing me all the time, Robyn thought with a kind of whimsical irony. If she had known what she was being assessed for...but it didn't make any difference now. Considering his own...genes, David's judgement of her was very flattering, but she had never thought of making such a scientific selection for the fathering of her child.

She hadn't really thought of what she would do; the idea of having a child outside marriage had only come to her tonight—certainly not considered in any intimate detail. Although she had spoken the truth about wanting to have a child of her own one day.

'He's very excited about it, the thought of having a child, with you as its mother,' Julian said jerkily, emotion furring his voice. 'It will make these next few months bearable, knowing that...knowing that his child might go on from where he left off. His life is not all wasted. He can die happy if...'

He bent his head and Robyn saw his throat working convulsively. 'It sounds very cold-blooded,' he said huskily. 'It's not, really. Davey wants this, quite desperately. I would do anything to help him.'

His head came up and there was naked pleading in his eyes. 'Offering you money was not the way to persuade you. I can see that now, Robyn. But money does take away a lot of problems in life, and you can have as much of it as you like. And I'll look after you and the child, smooth every path. I'll make it as easy for you as I can. I swear to you I will do all this, if you have Davey's child.'

The tug on her heart was all the stronger for what he promised—to be taken care of for the rest of her life. It wasn't the money, she knew she could always support herself, but the feeling that he would always be there, ready to answer her call, caring about what happened to her...and the child, of course. Her child, as well as David's.

Robyn had no solid reason to trust Julian Lassiter. Yet she did. She believed, without any shadow of a doubt, that he would carry out precisely what he promised. She could depend on him and he would never let her down. What he now gave to his brother, he would extend to her. She would belong to him.

Then a breath of cold reality chilled the warm substance of that thought. She would belong to Julian's family, but not to him. David was the man she had to give herself to in the act of conception. She would have to accept him into her bed and let him...do what had to be done to make her pregnant.

Could she go through with it?

Did she really want to go through with it?

She looked at Julian and couldn't say the no that hovered on her lips. 'Give me a day to consider it. It's...it's a big decision.'

He nodded, disappointed, but taking some comfort in the postponement. He reached over and took her hand, pressing it in an expression of deep feeling. 'I'm very grateful to you for the sympathetic way you've listened, Robyn. I hope the answer will be yes, but if not, I appreciate the consideration anyway. And I'm sorry my superficial judgement of you...was so hopelessly wrong.'

He sighed and rose to his feet, his gaze dropping to the pamphlets on the coffee-table. 'Have you made any definite plans for tomorrow?'

'No. I was thinking of a helicopter ride, but...' She shrugged and stood up to see him out.

'Let me take you.'

She knew he wanted her answer. Time was running out for David Lassiter. It was cruel to keep him waiting, but it was her life too, her body.

'I'll ring you in the morning,' Julian pressed.

'Yes. All right.' She nodded.

They walked to the door. He opened it, paused, glanced back, his eyes boring straight to her heart. 'Tomorrow.'

'Yes,' she whispered.

And he left her alone with her thoughts, thoughts that echoed the title of one of Gauguin's most memorable Polynesian paintings: *Where do we come from? What are we? Where are we going?*

CHAPTER SIX

ROBYN was early. It was still a few minutes short of nine-fifteen, but Julian was there waiting for her in the lobby. He stood by one of the huge *cloisonné* vases that flanked the entrance to the hotel. They were made of enamelled brass and covered with beautiful floral scrolls and symbols. Julian appeared to be studying the intricate patterns.

Robyn paused in her step, wondering how the night had passed for him. And David. Julian looked tired. He had made no reference to the proposition when he had telephoned her earlier this morning to say he had booked them on a helicopter flight at ten o'clock. Robyn felt sure he would respect her need for time and not press a decision, but it weighed heavily on her mind. And heart.

To involve herself in such a painful situation was against all common sense. She had made up her mind to back out of it this morning...until he had called. And then she couldn't do it. Not coldly over the telephone. She didn't know why she cared so much about what he felt. She hadn't even thought about what David would feel. It was Julian.

His head lifted sharply and his gaze swung around as if he had sensed her presence. His face relaxed into a welcoming smile when he spotted her, and Robyn moved forward to meet him, her pulse hammering at this evidence of warmth from him.

He was dressed conservatively in a white shirt and grey trousers, but Julian Lassiter didn't need colourful clothes to make an impact. In every idyllic sense of the word, he was a man—provider, protector, hunter—and everything about him proclaimed he was in command.

But he hadn't been in command last night, Robyn amended swiftly. He had shown such deep feelings—passionate need, despair, love. Nevertheless, she could not blind herself to that other side of him, the hard, cynical, ruthless side. Was she mad to trust him? What was the real heart of the man?

He was not unaware that he had an effect on her. She had admitted as much before they left the dinner-table last night. He could be using his emotion to play on hers, appealing to her humane instincts, manipulating her into doing what he wanted for his brother. And then... but he would do as he promised. His word was his bond. Hadn't he implied that to David yesterday? She was sure it was true.

'I have a taxi waiting,' he said, and swept Robyn straight outside.

The taxi-driver was chatting to a bellboy, but he snapped to attention the moment he saw Julian and quickly opened the passenger door for Robyn. As Julian settled beside her, Robyn was forcibly reminded of the feelings she had experienced in the taxi yesterday, but the parameters had subtly changed. He was still invading her personal space, but there was now a compelling attraction about having him beside her, looking after her, smoothing the path.

It was a ten-minute drive to the heliport. Julian did not speak. Neither did Robyn. Her mind and emotions were at war. The taxi-driver rattled on about features of the resort that they passed. Robyn idly wondered if all the taxi-drivers on Maui were compulsive talkers, or if providing tourist information was part of their working-rules.

The taxi turned into a pineapple plantation and the driver apologised for the rough route, but it was the only way up to the hill where the heliport was situated. He plunged on with a talk about the cultivation of pine-apples as they wound their way up.

The heliport did not cover a large area. Two heli-copters sat on the mown lawns outside an office building and, just as the taxi pulled into the small car park, a line of five passengers was led out to one of them. Julian arranged with the taxi-driver to call back at eleven o'clock for them and they stepped out into a gusty wind.

Robyn was glad she had worn a long-sleeved blouse with her blue slacks. The air was considerably cooler here, and would undoubtedly be a great deal cooler when they flew over the Haleakala Crater. The dormant volcano was the largest in the world, rising to over ten thousand feet.

Julian steered her into the office building where they had to register for their flight. Robyn noticed that theirs were the only two names written down for the ten o'clock de-luxe trip around the island, and the office-girl's manner to Julian was very deferential, offering drinks of coffee or fruit-punch while they waited, signalling for a work-mate who immediately left his paperwork to ex-plain to them how they should board the helicopter, warning against going near the tail, and instructing them about the seat-belts and earphones.

He ushered them out to the viewing-deck and promised to return to guide them the moment their helicopter landed from its current tour. 'Isn't there anyone else joining us for this trip?' Robyn asked as he was about to leave them.

He glanced in surprise at Julian, who answered for him. 'I booked the helicopter for us.'

Robyn looked at him incredulously. She knew from the pamphlet how much the de-luxe trip cost per person, and she had seen five people go out to the helicopter which had taken off while they were registering. And, for all she knew, that number might not be a full complement of passengers.

'Why?' she asked, unable to justify such extravagance.

His eyes held hers with steady relentless purpose. 'I didn't want to share it with anyone else.'

The power of the man closed around her, drawing her towards a surrender she was not yet prepared to make. 'You're quite ruthless when you're going after something you want, aren't you?' she observed.

'When it's for someone I love, yes. Entirely ruthless,' he answered unequivocally.

Someone he loved . . . the thought lingered in her mind as Robyn turned away from him. He would love David's child—she knew that for a certainty—but how would *she* feel? That was the question. Could she cope with what had to happen first?

'You don't even like me,' she said with sharp irony.

He studied her for a moment, his eyes carefully devoid of expression. 'I did apologise for yesterday. And last night. I was wrong. And there is much that I do like about you, Robyn,' he answered as if he was choosing his words with deliberate tact and precision.

'You say that you will always be available to help. What of your own life, Julian?' she asked, needing to know more about him.

'My life . . .' His mouth twisted sardonically. 'It's not worth much, regardless of what Davey said. I work. I play golf. Occasionally I meet with friends. Entertain business associates. If I died tomorrow it wouldn't matter. I wish it were me instead of Davey.'

He really meant it. Robyn could see that. 'What about...other personal involvements?' She meant women, and he knew it.

The weary cynicism flashed back into his eyes. 'A casual relationship now and then. Meaningless.' There was a flicker of curiosity. 'What about you?'

'I was engaged to be married once. It didn't work out,' she replied, disinclined to tell him how recent the disillusionment was.

His lips curled. 'Better not to get married than to...' He bit off the words, compressing his mouth into a line of grim bitterness before turning away to stare out over the landscape.

Than to what? Robyn wondered. To love and lose? How much had his wife meant to him? He had been hurt...wounded...perhaps more deeply than she had ever been. She didn't try to probe. It didn't really have any bearing on the situation. The only real question was whether she would marry David and have his child.

She leaned on the veranda railing and gazed out towards the coastline where a row of tall pine-trees separated land from sea. She could go on being an island, answerable to no one but herself, or she could cast herself into a sea of unknowns, with Julian Lassiter as a bulwark against whatever tribulations arose.

She didn't need that, she argued. But somehow her independence didn't seem all that attractive any more. It felt more lonely than ever.

A helicopter came in to land. Six passengers disembarked. The man came out of the office and signalled for Robyn and Julian to follow him. Robyn was handed into the seat next to the pilot and Julian climbed in beside her. The pilot smiled at them and indicated the seat-belts and earphones. It was impossible to hear anything above the sound of the machine. As soon as they were ready, the helicopter lifted off the ground.

The curved front window afforded them a hundred-and-eighty-degrees view, which was all very fine, but as they swooped away from the heliport Robyn's stomach lurched at the sensation of having only a pane of glass between herself and the ground below. As if he had sensed her nervousness, Julian took her hand, imparting a comforting reassurance with the warm strength of his.

She glanced gratefully at him and he smiled at her— the first real smile she had seen from him—and it curled around Robyn's heart, squeezing it. She wrenched her gaze away to stare out of the window in front of her. But the landscape below was only a mish-mash of patterns until she found the strength of mind really to focus on it.

The pilot introduced himself and proceeded to point out various landmarks. The words blurred into Robyn's mind. Her eyes turned on cue to the majestic mountains of West Maui with their sharply cut valleys; the cane-fields on the plains—one had been set alight and a trail of smoke was weaving upwards; the rocky coastline of little bays; she saw everything, but her awareness was centred on the hand still holding hers.

She could have broken the hold, pulled away, but she didn't. She wondered if Julian knew what he was doing...if he was deliberately impressing on her that they would be joined together in the lifelong enterprise that would begin if she agreed to the proposition.

The realisation hammered through her heart that Julian Lassiter would walk out of her life as abruptly as he had come into it...if she rejected his brother. And what was David thinking now? David, whose brilliance was facing extinction for ever, who had laid this burden at her feet either to pick up or to step over and walk away.

They rose through cloud to the summit of Haleakala. On the black edge of the crater were a group of buildings and the silver domes of observatories. 'Science City,' the pilot informed them as they started the descent into the great pit of the volcano.

It was an eerie landscape. Wisps of cloud drifted around patches of violet rocks. Swards of olive green grass swept down from the cliff edges, but in the vast centre were waves of small craters, pitted hillocks of fine dust hued from a simmering orange to yellow ochre, and every shade therefrom down to the white-grey of ashes. It was a fantastic sight, yet faintly chilling in its deathlike atmosphere. Here was the aftermath of destructive forces that obliterated life.

Even as the words crept into her mind, Robyn glanced at Julian and he spoke them. She couldn't hear him but she could lip-read what he was saying: 'Ashes to ashes, dust to dust.' And the pain in his eyes was testament enough to what he was thinking.

David... only three more months... maybe six.

Robyn squeezed his hand, wanting to comfort, wanting to help, wanting to ease the pain that wished he could give his life for his brother's. And Robyn realised in that instant that she had the one power he didn't have, couldn't have. The power to give birth to life. Julian would do what he asked of her, if he could. Couldn't she do it for his sake... for David?

It awaited all of them—the wasteland of death—and Robyn looked at her life and asked herself if it was really worth anything. Possibly she had contributed some enjoyment to the lives of other people. But she hadn't added to the precious store of human knowledge that could save lives, as David had done, was continuing to do by allowing himself to be used as a medical experiment. The waste of a mind like that...

To bear his child, perhaps a child that would have David's abilities, wouldn't that be worth doing? If she could lift her mind off the mechanics that would achieve that end, and just hold on to that concept, surely she could go through with it. And Julian would always be there, ready to hold her hand whenever her courage looked like failing her.

Robyn didn't know when they flew away from the crater. They passed by jungle-clad cliffs and waterfalls with pools that created liquid steps to the sea. The pilot pointed out the hamlet of Hana and other settlements, the residences and ranches of old and new celebrities, the various plantations, the international airport...and yesterday was another life ago.

They swept into Waiehu Valley where the almost vertical walls of the West Maui mountains rose to over three thousand feet. The helicopter wove down a ravine. They hovered in space, waterfalls all around them, hurtling sheets of water, the gift of life to the dead land of the volcano, regeneration, the future.

And it was then that Robyn made up her mind. She would go through with it. Do as Julian proposed. The reasons were too complex to analyse properly. It had more to do with feelings. And, having made the decision, she felt a peace and contentment she had never before experienced.

They landed back at the heliport. Julian helped her out. He did not release her hand. They walked away from the helicopter together and when the noise of the machine had receded enough for her to speak and be heard, she stopped walking and turned to the man who had promised always to stand by her and her child.

She felt more vulnerable in that moment than she had ever done before in her adult life. Julian sensed her answer even before she spoke, and his free hand lifted and touched her face with a tender salute.

'I'll do it...for him...because maybe our child...will be like him. Or our child's child. At least David won't be lost, will he?'

'No, he won't be lost,' Julian agreed softly. His fingers gently stroked the hair back from her forehead with the loving, reassuring touch of a brother to a little sister. 'Do you remember what the taxi-driver said about the meaning of *aloha*?'

'Yes,' she whispered, her voice barely husking over the lump of emotion that had risen in her throat. 'Love, mercy, compassion...'

'I was thinking of the old Hawaiian greeting—"Eye to eye, face to face, I greet you and give to you my peace, in fact, the very breath of life,"' Julian recited as if he had nursed the words in his heart.

His eyes caressed her soul. 'What you do is such a huge gift. And it will not be easy to be an "*aloha* bride", Robyn. But I shall help you in every way I can.'

Tears brimmed her eyes and trickled down her cheeks. Julian stepped forward and wrapped her in his arms. Reaction quivered through Robyn as she surrendered herself to his keeping. Julian gently pressed her head on to his broad shoulder and held her tight, cocooning her in his warmth until the shivering stopped.

'I'll be with you, Robyn,' he assured her quietly. 'You won't be alone in this, I promise you. Anything you want or need, you have only to call me and tell me.'

She closed her eyes and savoured the strength she was leaning on. To be held like this, to be told she could always count on him, to feel so safe in his embrace... Robyn felt that this was what she had been looking for all her life. If the price to have Julian looking after her was to be an '*aloha* bride' to his brother, then she would gladly pay that price.

CHAPTER SEVEN

THE taxi was waiting for them. The driver had obviously witnessed their embrace. It was impossible to know what he had deduced from it, but he didn't bother chattering on as he drove them back to the hotel.

Neither Robyn nor Julian spoke. They were both deeply sunk in their own thoughts.

The ten-minute drive seemed to take for ever.

Had she made the right decision? Robyn fretted. She had come here on a holiday—to enjoy herself. Not even twenty-four hours had passed, and she was deeply involved with problems that were not her own. The pattern she had set for her life was all awry, and the need to get back in control of it clawed through her mind.

The taxi finally arrived at the hotel and she and Julian quickly alighted. It was he who spoke first. 'Robyn, take a few more hours to think about this. I'll go up to my room, give you the opportunity to change your mind.'

Robyn turned to him, wondering if he knew how much his presence had influenced her decision. And, even as her eyes met his, she knew she would go through with it. But the time to think it all through . . . yes, she needed that. 'Thank you,' she said in a voice she hardly recognised as her own. It wobbled with uncertainties.

His eyes stabbed into her, looking for a steadfastness that matched his own. 'If I haven't heard otherwise from you by three o'clock, I'll tell Davey your answer is yes,' he said, reminding her that time was an urgent factor where his brother was concerned.

'Agreed,' she said more firmly, hoping to have herself sorted out by then.

'If your answer is yes, Robyn,' he continued relentlessly, 'then keep this afternoon free. I'll be taking you to the Maui Memorial Hospital at Wailuku. In order to get married here, it's necessary for you to have a blood test for rubella—German measles. That takes a day. We can then get the marriage licence. You and Davey can be married tomorrow afternoon.'

Robyn had a moment's trepidation at this further evidence of the efficient ruthlessness of the man. 'Were you so confident that I would say yes, that you found all this out, Julian?'

'Not at all,' he confessed with an apologetic smile. 'I was expecting you to turn the proposition down. But I couldn't disregard the possibility, and with Davey...' the smile faded, swallowed up by the dark pressure of an illness that was beyond his control '...time is of the essence.'

'Of course,' Robyn murmured, but although she had agreed to the marriage, she hadn't anticipated the speed with which she would be rushed into it. The need to think it all through was even more pressing now.

'I'll call you before three o'clock,' she assured him, and turned away, walking quickly through the atrium and taking the first path she came to that led down through the grounds.

She walked because the physical rhythm of movement always seemed to jog her mind into sharper working order. Right now a destination didn't matter. The path led on to another path that followed the beach-front to the next hotel, and the next, but nothing around her made any impression on Robyn.

Pain, the old lady had said—strange how that prediction kept popping into her mind. She wasn't marrying Julian at all. She had violently rejected the idea last night, but she wished now that it was his baby he wanted her to have.

Instead she had been drawn into the commitment of having a child by a man who had only a few months to live. But a child was all he was asking of her. No living together. The marriage was only a legality.

The question was, how to avoid becoming emotionally involved with what remained of David's life? Robyn knew herself too well to doubt that, the more she saw of him, the more involved she would become with what he was suffering through.

And there was the pain!

It would tear her life apart.

And no, she couldn't accept that. Wouldn't accept it. The child, yes. She would do that for him, because he was the man he was, and because she wanted Julian Lassiter to stay in her life. But she had to set some predetermined limits to the situation. Conditions that she could cope with. And still it would not be easy.

If a child was to be conceived... Her whole body clenched at the thought of what had to happen first. It took considerable will-power to reason herself out of the emotional reaction.

She was bound to freeze up—even with Larry it hadn't been easy to relax—but that didn't matter. She didn't have to feel any pleasure in the act. David wouldn't be expecting anything more than acquiescence. They were only coming together to create a life. It was something good, something worth while.

She would just have to block her mind to everything else and think of the end—a baby of her own to hold and love, a child who would never want for anything if Julian kept his promises. And he would. She knew he would. He would always be there.

And what was necessary with David...if they were to be married tomorrow...Robyn mentally revised what the doctor had told her when she had gone to discuss contraception, and felt intensely relieved when she realised that the next few days were the most likely time for her to get pregnant. If she was lucky, the most difficult part of the agreement would be quickly fulfilled.

By the time she returned to her room, Robyn had determined on the conditions she would set. She tried very hard not to think of how either of the Lassiter men might react to them. It was the only way that she was prepared to carry it through.

Julian answered her telephone-call on the first ring and Robyn could hear the tension in his voice as he quickly identified himself.

'It's Robyn,' she said just as quickly. 'There are a few things I want to have cleared up before we settle this, Julian.'

'Go ahead,' he invited.

'At the moment I'm not personally involved with David and I prefer it to remain that way.'

'I understand that. Of course.'

Robyn took a deep breath. 'As I see it, we only have to meet for the marriage ceremony. Apart from that, I'll let you know what nights he is to come to my room.'

'That's fine, Robyn. Anything else?'

'No. You can tell him yes, under those conditions.'

'They're accepted without question. And thank you, Robyn. I...' She heard his sharp intake of breath, and when he continued his voice was furred with deep emotion. 'I don't know what else to say to you. Thank you seems so inadequate.'

'Don't! Don't say anything!' she cried, clamping down on a frightening well of response to his emotion. 'When do you want to leave for the hospital?'

There was a slight pause, then a return to brisk efficiency. 'Give me half an hour.'

'Fine. I'll meet you in the lobby.'

Robyn's hand was trembling as she put the telephone down. Sheer, mindless fear was thumping through her heart. She didn't know why, but suddenly it felt all wrong, what she had just done, and all her carefully thought out reasoning was no comfort at all.

But it was what Julian wanted her to do, had begged her to do. She didn't have a choice. It was the only way. So it had to be all right. Had to be. And she mustn't think about it any more. It was done. Irrevocable. Julian had given her the chance to change her mind, and it was too late to change it back now. He would never forgive her if she did.

And she didn't know why that should mean so much to her, either. But it did. Julian would be telling his brother the good news this very minute, and he was counting on her to keep to her word. She couldn't let him down. Besides which, it had always been a point of honour with Robyn never to let anyone down once she had given her word. She knew how that felt. It had happened to her all too often.

Bit by bit Robyn patched back her composure. By the time she had to meet Julian for the trip to the hospital she was relatively calm. And Julian couldn't see the nerves that played havoc with her empty stomach as he took her arm and led her out to a stretch limousine.

Robyn had never ridden in such a car. The seats were plush, the leg-room unbelievable, and the distance from the driver so great that it emphasised the fact that they were travelling in state.

First a whole helicopter, now a stretch limousine! She sent Julian a dry smile. 'You do like your comfort, don't you?'

'It's not a matter of comfort, but of privacy,' he replied, his eyes wary of causing offence as he added, 'There are things we have to talk about, Robyn. The settlement, various arrangements, the future.'

She wrenched her eyes away as a painful flush burnt up her throat. 'I'm not doing it for the money,' she muttered tightly.

'I know that,' he said softly. He reached over and took her hand, pressing it to draw her attention back to him. His eyes begged her forgiveness. 'I was so wrong about you, it's forced me to re-think. In the years since my wife...died...' He shook his head. 'Davey's right. I've been allowing a personal grief, and bitterness, to warp my judgement.'

He squeezed her hand and his warm admiration washed over Robyn, soothing the hurt he had previously inflicted. 'You have shown me the kind of giving that I never believed a woman capable of. A depth of caring, and compassion...' The admiration crystallised into burning purpose. 'Believe me, you'll never hear a harsh word from me again, Robyn. Nor will I tolerate or permit any criticism of you from anyone. What you're doing for Davey...it's out of the ordinary. Beyond most people's comprehension. You must call on me if anything upsets you. At any time, Robyn. I mean that. The Lassiters look after their own.'

The fiercely protective note, the possessive way he linked her with his family... Robyn suddenly felt a sense of security that her own family had never imparted. 'Thank you,' she said, not caring in that moment what anyone else might think of what she was doing.

Their eyes locked, and for a moment—a brief, power-charged moment—something leapt between them that was warmer than admiration, warmer than gratitude—something that they instantly and instinctively drew back from. Robyn dropped her lashes. Julian jerked his head around to look out of the side window. His thumb rubbed agitatedly over her knuckles. Her pulse skipped through several beats in an erratic fashion.

'Davey has arranged for a solicitor to come to the hotel this evening,' Julian said tightly, and when his gaze swung back to her his eyes were bleak, his face grimly set in its lines of command.

'His estate will go into a trust for the child,' he continued matter-of-factly. 'I'll be the executor. You'll draw an income from the trust, but any other needs that come up will always be met. A house, car, education—whatever. You must understand, Robyn, as Davey's wife, you're entitled to this. It's Davey's will.'

Robyn did not argue. Julian was right. She had agreed to marry his brother... to have David's child. Julian would be her brother-in-law, her friend and confidant. She couldn't allow herself to think of him in any other way. But there was a sudden ache in her heart that was very close to pain.

Julian withdrew his hand from hers, ostensibly to make a gesture of extending his support. 'I'll appoint someone from my staff to help you with your business. Do the legwork when it becomes awkward for you.'

'That's not necessary,' Robyn cut in quickly, almost snapping from the tension between them. 'I've always handled things myself and...'

'But when you're pregnant...' Julian frowned anxiously at her. 'You must let me take care of you, Robyn.'

'It's my business, and I can work my own hours, Julian,' she insisted with a flash of proud independence. It upset her—quite unreasonably—to think it was the child he wanted to look after, and not her. 'You don't have to... to nursemaid me.'

He studied the mutinous set of her face for a moment, then retreated. 'We'll see,' he muttered.

Robyn wondered if he ever conceded defeat when he set his mind on something. But at least he was on her side now. And did it really matter if it was only for the child's sake? In this situation, what more could she expect than what he had promised her—loyalty, security, protection? And Julian would never let her down. He would deliver what he promised.

The ache in her heart eased a little.

But Robyn could not help envying the woman who had been Julian's wife. He must have loved her very much to have been so wounded by her death. And how had she died? Was it because he had been unable to prevent it that Julian was bitter? Robyn desperately wanted to ask, but Julian forestalled the temptation with another question.

'There's no chance of your having German measles, is there?'

Robyn stifled a sigh. 'No. I was inoculated against it in my teens.'

'Have you any objection to the marriage being held in Davey's room?' he asked cautiously.

'No.'

'I'll let you know the time as soon as I've got it organised.'

'Thank you.'

They arrived at the hospital and the next half-hour was taken up with clinical officialdom. Robyn wished she had thought to eat something before she left the hotel. She felt quite faint by the time Julian escorted her back to the limousine.

She decided to order a room-service meal as soon as she got back to her room. The thought of dressing up and going out to a restaurant was beyond contemplation in her present state of mind. Was it only last night that she had gone to Swan Court?

She looked dazedly at Julian.

He caught her gaze and frowned. 'I was wondering about your family,' he asked in sharp concern. 'How will they react?'

'They'll think it strange,' Robyn answered slowly. What was happening was strange to her, and she couldn't explain it even to herself. It was as if she had stepped into an entirely different life. 'I doubt they'll really be upset. I'm something of an outsider in my family.' She shrugged as Julian's frown deepened. 'They're involved in their own lives,' she added dismissively.

'But don't they care about you?' Julian asked. He looked shocked.

Did they care? she wondered. The kid sister who'd been a nuisance to them? The daughter who was one child too many? Never close, like Julian and David. 'In a way, I suppose they do. A blood-relative is more or less taken for granted. They'll probably be shocked at first, but it won't make any difference to our relationship,' she said with weary certainty.

Robyn privately vowed that she would be close to her child. As close as any mother and child could be. It would be one satisfying relationship to fill that vacuum in her life.

'I need your ring size,' Julian said decisively. 'We'll do this thing properly. No one else has to know it's merely a legality. Certainly not your family.'

He was intent on protecting her. Robyn appreciated the thought and didn't argue. She glanced down at her bare hands. 'I don't know what size. I've never bought rings.'

'I noticed a jeweller in the hotel—first shop along Lahaina corridor. Go there tomorrow morning and have the size measured. I'll give them your name so they'll be expecting you, and I'll buy something appropriate for the ceremony.'

'All right,' she nodded, then turned to him curiously. 'What about your family, Julian? What are they going to think about this?'

'There's only my father and Janet, Davey's mother. I'll handle them,' he said with the air of ruthless efficiency that was so much part of the man.

Head of the Lassiter Corporation, Robyn reminded herself. But he had heart too, and it was the heart she wanted, to be gathered into the fold of his caring. And that was why she was marrying David, Robyn suddenly realised. The main reason.

Maybe...one day...but first there was David, and nothing was going to change that. A deep sadness settled into her soul.

The greatest sadness, the old lady had said.

Robyn shook her head. Was she to be haunted by that prediction for the rest of her life?

It was a relief to part from Julian back at the hotel. By agreeing to become David's wife and bear his child, she might have become a very special woman in Julian's eyes—one he had vowed to take care of—but that was all. It was stupid to imagine—or want—more from him.

Once back in her room, Robyn didn't leave it. She ordered a meal, did her best to force it down, then watched television until she was tired enough to go to bed. She didn't want to think, and mercifully sleep came quickly, blanketing the pain that hadn't gone away. She slept for a long time.

The buzzing of the telephone woke her at nine o'clock the next morning. It was Julian, telling her the marriage ceremony was set for four o'clock that afternoon. He would come and take her up to Davey's room after the Justice of the Peace had arrived.

'Thank you,' she half slurred, still drugged with sleep.

'Are you all right, Robyn?'

The concerned note in his voice hurt. 'Yes. Fine. I'll see you at four, then.'

'Robyn.' His steady tone sounded strained. 'Is there anything you'd like me to do for you? Anything you want today?'

'No. No, thank you, Julian. I'll be ready,' she said quickly, and hung up.

Robyn sat staring blankly at the telephone, clenching her hands as she fought down panic. I'm not going to think about it, she recited to herself over and over again. I'm just going to do it. A few days...that was all it was. And thank God the time was right, so there'd be no waiting for the nights that had to be got through.

She showered and dressed in a light cotton shift, then went straight down to the Pavilion for breakfast. It was an informal restaurant situated near one end of the swimming-pool. Robyn sat at one of the outside tables that were shaded by huge straw umbrellas.

Although it was still quite early in the day, most of the loungers around the pool were occupied by guests soaking up the sun. Robyn felt oddly detached from the whole holiday scene. She told herself that there was nothing to stop her enjoying the various activities that were available for her pleasure, but she could not work up enough enthusiasm actually to plan something. Tomorrow, she promised herself. Tomorrow when the worst was over.

She was trying to eat a breakfast dish of tropical fruits when she remembered about the jeweller, but she didn't hurry. There was plenty of time. Too much time. Eventually she walked through the Japanese garden and entered Lahaina corridor from the far end of the building.

She stopped to buy a bestseller paperback at one of the shops. Perhaps it would fill in the hours.

She lingered through the art gallery which featured many local artists as well as prints of more famous artists' paintings. Would Julian's home contain famous originals? she wondered. Did he live alone, or had he gone back to live with his father and stepmother since he was widowed and childless? She reminded herself to ask him.

Robyn thought of her small terraced house in Paddington. It was far from luxurious, but it was handy to the business centre of Oxford Street and she had turned the ground-floor rooms into a smart place of business. The two bedrooms upstairs were somewhat spartan, but it wouldn't take too much work and money to turn the second bedroom into a nursery for the baby. A smile lightened the heavy burden in her mind. How she would love that baby!

Julian had called on the jeweller. As soon as Robyn gave her name at the counter of the elegant boutique the manager promptly came forward, treating her with the utmost deference as he tested her finger-size. He smiled at her as he noted it down.

'I'll have a selection ready for Mr Lassiter,' he assured her.

Robyn could have told him that a plain gold ring would suffice, but found the situation too embarrassing to discuss. She left it to Julian.

There was one other thing she had to do. She did her best to smother her sense of embarrassment and headed for the registration desk to ask for a duplicate key to her room, a key for David to use when he came to her to-night. She shrank from letting him in, talking. Better for her to be in bed with the lights out. Maybe that way she could cope without falling to pieces at the last moment.

The day passed with agonising slowness. Robyn was ready long before Julian knocked on her door at five minutes to four. In deference to the fact that she was getting married—an extraordinary occasion in more ways than one—she had put on her favourite yellow dinner-dress: a simple affair with a soft blouson bodice, a white leather belt that curved down at the front of her trim waist and featured an enamel daisy, and a skirt that fitted snugly over her hips before swinging out into graceful gores. She had strapped on the white high-heeled sandals which went with every dress she had brought with her, and tucked the extra room-key into her white handbag. Her short blonde hair had been washed and brushed into shape. Some judicious make-up added some colour to her pale face. She had even revarnished her nails a pearly coral colour to pass some time.

Robyn was satisfied that she looked composed, but when the expected knock came she took a long, deep breath before opening the door.

Julian was in his dark grey suit. A freshly made lei of frangipani flowers hung from his wrist. He smiled at her, a smile of encouraging approval.

Robyn could not return it. She stared at him, stiff-faced, the most terrible panic pounding through her heart. It was Julian she wanted. Julian! And he was giving her to his brother. Approving a marriage that should be as wrong to him as it was to her. She searched his eyes in frantic appeal. Didn't he even sense it was wrong?

He lifted the lei off his wrist and carefully positioned it around her neck. '*Aloha,* Robyn,' he murmured, his hands still resting on her shoulders. Then he leaned forward and kissed her forehead. 'This is a fine thing you do. Don't ever think otherwise,' he added in a husky whisper.

Robyn couldn't speak. She was fighting tears.

Julian took a small velvet bag out of his jacket pocket, extracted a ring, took her left hand and slid a dazzling solitaire diamond on to her third finger. 'And this is from Davey. In appreciation.'

'No. I...' She choked. Julian couldn't possibly feel what she felt for him. He couldn't do this if he did. And she couldn't pull away from him now. It was too late. Somehow she had become irrevocably tied to his will, and she had to do what he wanted.

'It's little enough for what you do for him,' Julian insisted gravely. 'Accept it, Robyn.'

She nodded, too wrought up to argue. Julian took her arm and walked her up to the lifts. Neither of them spoke. Robyn felt an eerie resignation...like the

Hawaiian princess who had been chosen as a sacrifice to the God of the volcano, an *aloha* garland around her neck, allowing herself to be calmly led to her doom.

The sweet smell of the frangipani was almost suffocating as they rode upwards in the small compartment. Robyn thought it would haunt her for the rest of her life.

As she had expected, David's room was on one of the Regency Club floors with a magnificent ocean view. A space had been cleared near the glass doors which opened on to the balcony. Robyn was introduced to the Justice of the Peace and two of the hotel staff who were standing in as witnesses. She took her place beside David.

The ceremony was short. Robyn forced her voice to make the right responses. David held her hand. He had long, supple fingers like Julian's. Even his voice sounded like Julian's. He slid the wedding ring on her finger, next to the diamond. They signed a paper.

'Robyn...' He said her name softly, caringly.

She lifted her eyes to his, reluctantly, fearfully.

They were so clear, those green eyes, clear and far-seeing and sure. He lifted his hand to her cheek in a tender salute that strangely echoed the gesture Julian had made when she had first given him her answer.

'Thank you,' he said with direct simplicity, but the words were heavy with feeling.

'I wish you well, David,' she managed to get out.

He smiled. 'And I you. Go now.' He dropped his hand and lifted his clear gaze to Julian. 'I give you into my brother's keeping.'

Julian took her arm and steered her away, out of David's room and into an adjoining one. A trolley was set with afternoon tea and Julian led her to a chair. 'I thought you might feel in need of some refreshment. Tea or coffee? Or would you prefer a stiff drink?'

Robyn did not sit down. She couldn't stay with Julian. She couldn't bear to be with him when she had to be David's wife tonight. She opened her handbag and drew out the key.

'Thank you, but I'd rather go, if you don't mind,' she said, deliberately not meeting his eyes as she held out the key to him. 'Please give this to David. Tell him...tell him that tonight is appropriate. He can come at ten o'clock. The lights will be out. I...I prefer it that way.'

He took the key, turning it over and over in his hand instead of putting it away. 'Robyn...' His voice gravelled over her name.

'No, please, don't say anything. Thank you for all you've done,' she said quickly. She flashed him a desperate little smile and strode for the door as fast as her shaky legs could move.

He didn't try to detain her. She went back to her room and cried into the lei that Julian had given her. Eventually she mopped up her tears, ordered a room-service dinner, ate what she could of it, tidied up her room, undressed, showered again and slipped on the *yukata*, trying not to think of her nakedness beneath it.

The hotel maid came in to turn down the bed. She put a flower on the top sheet and wished Robyn a good night. Robyn picked up the flower and placed it beside the lei on the coffee-table. She settled on the sofa to watch television until the appointed hour.

One programme followed another. Robyn didn't really see or hear a thing, but she was very conscious of the time ticking away. At nine-thirty she switched the television off, went to the bathroom, then cleaned her teeth with unnecessary vigour.

One by one she turned off the lights. She took off the *yukata* and laid it on the end of the bed. The sheets felt very cold as she slid between them. She watched the luminous numbers of the clock on the bedside-table.

Aloha, she thought. I give you my peace, in fact, the very breath of life.

That was what she had to remember and hold tight to her heart.

Aloha.

CHAPTER EIGHT

THE 10:00 figures were still showing red on the digital clock when the door clicked open and shut. Robyn couldn't bring herself to move, to turn over and face him. Her eyes clung desperately to the luminous numerals. Her mind feverishly told her that by ten-thirty he would be gone. Sooner if possible.

He sat on the bed. The top sheet tightened over her body with his weight pulling it down. A hand gently touched her shoulder. 'I know how distasteful this must be.' His voice was gruff, indistinct.

Robyn shut her eyes tight. Her heart pounded into mad life. It sounded like Julian's voice. Yet that was impossible. She had to be wrong. The aching need to have Julian was distorting her senses. It had to be David who was with her. Any other conclusion only demonstrated the wildness of her imagination. But she could pretend it was Julian who was making love to her. Then it wouldn't be so terrible.

A hand drew the sheet down her body and Robyn had a moment's horror at the unexpected exposure of her nakedness. But it was dark, she frantically reasoned, and the next instant strong arms were folding her into a comforting embrace as he lay down beside her.

She was intensely grateful that he still had his clothes on. It made the shock of contact less frightening. A feather-light caress ran across the back of her neck. Her skin crawled with sensitivity and she fiercely wished she had worn a nightie. But it was too late now, and, swiftly

94

deciding she was as ready as she would ever be, Robyn
gathered the will-power to roll on to her back. As she
started to move, his arms tightened in resistance.

'Stay.'

The command—more breathed than spoken—ar-
rested the movement. She lifted her head, her eyes trying
vainly to probe the darkness for the likeness of his face.
Surely the strength of the arms that held her could not
belong to a sick and dying man. And yet...she had to
be wrong.

The need to know—to reassure her disordered senses—
drove her own hand to move, to slide experimentally over
his shoulder—so strongly muscled—his biceps no less
so. She grazed her fingers across the breadth of his back.
He shuddered under the lightness of her touch and she
felt the rippling play of more firmly fleshed muscles.

Could this really be David's body? She remembered
seeing the two brothers side by side—the same build—
and only the colouring had been starkly different.

He began stroking her back, slowly, sensuously, an
unhurried touch that left Robyn quivering in the wake
of those soft, caring fingertips that did not want to rush,
but seemed intent on making her feel wanted and needed
and desired.

Conflicting emotions raged through her. She wanted
the magic touch to go on, but there was not supposed
to be any pleasure from this act. She had not anticipated
it...expected only to have to endure what had to be done,
not to be caressed into a mindless and compelling sense
of being loved.

Perhaps David did feel love for her. It had to be him.
He was being kind, considerate, trying to make her feel
more relaxed. Yet Julian had called him calculating and
analytical. What he was doing to her could hardly be

called cold and calculating and analytical. It was warm and caring...and beautiful.

Was it possible that David had changed? After all, what could be more intensely personal than the desire to have a child? It wasn't unreasonable that he should feel at least a tenderness for her, for what she had agreed to do for him.

Before her inhibitions could check the impulse, Robyn pressed herself closer to him and reached up to curl her hand around his neck. His lips came to hers in a soft kiss of peace, then lingered, moving softly back and forth with a tingling sensuality that left Robyn entranced.

Without any conscious volition she found herself responding to the seductive movements of his mouth as if it were Julian, and with each changing contact and pressure she felt a growing excitement. He lowered her head to the pillow, and she was pricklingly aware of the muscled firmness of his chest pressing lightly over her breasts, but the distraction of his kiss, the sensations he was arousing on the sensitive inner tissues of her lips ... She opened her mouth to his sensual persuasion and was instantly catapulted into a dizzying spiral of wildly erotic excitement.

She didn't know why he drew such a wanton response from her...didn't think at all. His mouth possessed hers with a desperate passion that drove everything else from Robyn's mind. She clung to him, absorbing all the feeling he aroused in her and giving it back with the same sense of desperation.

His hand stroked down her body, stirring ripples of excitement. He pulled his clothes aside, and a wild quiver of anticipation spread through Robyn's stomach as she moved her legs to accommodate him. She wanted nothing to stop him now. It had to go on...be completed.

The more
you love romance . . .
the more
you'll love this offer

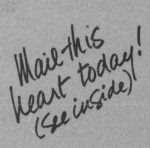

Mail this heart today! (See inside)

**Join us on a Harlequin Honeymoon
and we'll give you
4 free books
A free bracelet watch
And a free mystery gift**

IT'S A HARLEQUIN HONEYMOON— A SWEETHEART OF A FREE OFFER!

HERE'S WHAT YOU GET:

1. Four New Harlequin Presents® Novels—FREE!

Take a Harlequin Honeymoon with your four exciting romances—yours FREE from Harlequin Reader Service®. Each of these hot-off-the-press novels brings you the passion and tenderness of today's greatest love stories . . . your free passports to bright new worlds of love and foreign adventure.

2. A Lovely Bracelet Watch—FREE!

You'll love your elegant bracelet watch—this classic LCD quartz watch is a perfect expression of your style and good taste—and it is yours FREE as an added thanks for giving our Reader Service a try.

3. An Exciting Mystery Bonus—FREE!

You'll be thrilled with this surprise gift. It is elegant as well as practical.

4. Money-Saving Home Delivery!

Join Harlequin Reader Service® and enjoy the convenience of previewing eight new books every month delivered right to your home. Each book is yours for only $2.24*—26¢ less per book than the cover price. And there is *no* extra charge for postage and handling. Great savings plus total convenience add up to a sweetheart of a deal for you! If you're not completely satisfied, you may cancel at any time, for any reason, simply by sending us a note or shipping statement marked "cancel" or by returning any shipment to us at our cost.

5. Free Insiders' Newsletter

It's *heart to heart*®, the indispensible insiders' look at our most popular writers, upcoming books, even comments from readers and much more.

6. More Surprise Gifts

Because our home subscribers are our most valued readers, when you join the Harlequin Reader Service®, we'll be sending you additional free gifts from time to time—as a token of our appreciation.

START YOUR HARLEQUIN HONEYMOON TODAY—JUST COMPLETE, DETACH AND MAIL YOUR FREE-OFFER CARD

His breathing was as ragged as hers as he took her; and, like his kiss, there was no sudden invasion, but a gentle, caring pressure that her body welcomed and responded to with melting warmth. Her whole being felt poised on the edge of something unimaginable as he pushed forward. She heard him cry out in some unintelligible need, heard her own shuddering gasp at the fierce pleasure of feeling the fullness of him deep inside her. Her body arched up to his and writhed in wanton excitement before she could check the primitive impulse. Exquisite waves of feeling rippled through her, gathering a surging momentum that was almost frightening in its intensity. Muscles clenched in panicky resistance, but the tidal wave of sensation obliterated everything, draining all strength from her body and leaving her floating limply on a sea of mindless ecstasy.

Then she gave up caring what she did and let her body do as it willed; abetting every continuation of this incredible feeling, inciting him to lose control too, exulting in every contact, savouring every exquisite nuance of pleasure that could be extracted as long as it could go on; and her body wanted it to go on for ever.

But there came an end to it . . . a last flood of warm fulfilment . . . then his arms gathered her into a tight embrace, strong, secure, warmly comforting. She found herself weeping and didn't know why. A hand pressed her head on to a broad shoulder and stroked her hair.

Gradually her mind picked up wisps of thought and threaded them into a cohesive pattern that she instantly shied away from grasping. How could she respond to David—to any man—like that? How could she be lying contentedly in his arms as if he were a real lover?

All the cosy tenets of her life had been utterly shattered, destroyed by a passion so overwhelming that nothing else had existed for her. How could she go back to living contentedly in her old way, now that she knew...had been irrevocably taught a different reality? It was unbelievable that she had allowed this to happen to her, that David should drive her to a sensual climax that she had not even believed could happen with anyone!

A tremor of sheer horror ran through her. With an abruptness that startled him, she lifted herself out of his embrace and rolled to the edge of the bed, putting distance between them.

His hand curved over her shoulder, gently trying to draw her back.

'You must go now,' she choked out, her heart thumping painfully with the emotional torment of mixing up the two brothers in her mind. If it had been Julian, her response might have made sense...but David!

He made no immediate move. With mounting panic Robyn wondered if he would do as she had bidden him.

'Please,' she begged, flinching from any further contact.

Slowly, reluctantly, the hand dropped away. She heard him inhale and slowly exhale in a deep sigh. Robyn felt wretchedly miserable while he attended to his clothes. She had wanted the comforting sense of togetherness to go on too, to pretend a love which couldn't possibly exist. And if it did there was no possible hope for the future.

The purpose of his coming to her had been accomplished. At least for tonight.

Robyn felt a searing ache in her chest. She tried to summon up some words that might take the hard edge off her cold dismissal of the intimacy they had just shared.

'I'm sorry,' she blurted out. 'But I want to be alone now.'

Her words seemed to echo on, gathering a flock of ghastly overtones in the silence that followed them.

'Is it . . . too difficult for you?' His voice was muted, flat, all hint of emotion strained out of it, yet the inner torment from which the question had been torn was all too evident in the slight hesitation.

Shame swept through her. He had tried to make it good. The problem was, it had been *too* good. But she could hardly blame him for that. And she couldn't be certain that she had conceived tonight.

'I'll cope,' she said with more assurance than she felt. 'Somehow, some way, I'll cope. I have to.'

But the prospect was so daunting, Robyn quailed at her own words. She was being torn in two. Maybe after she had had some time to think about tonight she would be able to patch together some peace for herself.

The silence was even more dreadful before he answered her, and even then he could not control the tortured emotion that broke into his voice. 'Let us wait and see. I can't bear you to be so upset. Perhaps tonight was enough.'

'No!' She twisted around to face him in the dark, her heart wrenched in so many ways that only her commitment to him was clear to her. 'You must come,' she cried. 'I couldn't live with it if you didn't.'

'Can you live with it if I do?' he asked huskily, weighing her response against the tumult of emotions that throbbed through the darkness.

'I want the child,' she replied as steadily as she could. 'The rest is . . . is transitory.'

He leaned over and kissed her forehead. Just as Julian had done this afternoon when he'd placed the lei around her neck. It must run in the family, she thought in quiet despair.

Then with a quick motion of his body he was gone through the night, the door closing firmly behind him before Robyn could think what to do or say. Yet, after the primitive act that had been performed tonight, there wasn't much to be said or done, Robyn thought grimly, and felt an intense distaste for her incredible wantonness.

Her eyes caught the luminous numbers on the clock as she dropped back on to her pillow. Eleven forty-three. She stared at them in appalled disbelief. How long had she been caught up in that wild passion... how long had she spent being cradled against him, uncaring of the tangled intimacy of their bodies?

She had to put on a nightie, separate herself from the sensitivity that still lingered with her nakedness. She switched on the bedside-lamp and got up, almost running to the chest of drawers in the dressing-room. With feverish haste, she snatched out a modest cotton nightie and dragged it on, wanting, needing anything that might make her less conscious of the body which had proved to be such a stranger to her... a treacherous, unreliable stranger!

She snapped off the light and crawled back into bed, pulling the bedclothes up around her neck and huddling under them. For a long time she struggled to come to terms with what she had done, but it was impossible. She couldn't even excuse herself. It was not as if she had ever been a sexually orientated person. When she had submitted to Larry she had never lost control of herself. Her response to David Lassiter was totally inexplicable. And wrong! She barely knew the man!

She shook her head helplessly. If she kept thinking about it she would go mad. David... Julian... what did it matter now? It was done. Over for tonight. She shut her eyes and prayed for oblivion.

Eventually it came in the form of a restless sleep that at least granted her some hours' respite from conscious thought. No sooner was she fully awake than Robyn decided to leave the hotel for the day, avoiding all chance of meeting either of the Lassiters.

In her aching heart there was a blind belief that it was Julian who had made love to her, not David. Yet she was equally certain that, if she confronted them with that statement, there would be outright denial of the fact. Besides, it made no sense.

In an attempt to block the whole futile argument from her mind, Robyn caught a taxi down to Lahaina village, the historical township that had once been an important South Seas port for whalers in the nineteenth century. The taxi-driver set her down in Front Street, the main business centre which had kept its quaint and picturesque turn-of-the-century flavour.

But her heart wasn't in being there. She wandered around listlessly, without purpose, her life too disjointed to put any kind of motivation together.

The shops were all of painted clapboard; some with wooden floors and open-air windows on to the street; others with old-fashioned overhanging verandas on their second storey. The pavements were very narrow and busy. Most of the stores catered for the tourist with arts and crafts, coral, carved woods, and lots of the traditional scrimshaw, made of whale-bone but not by the sailors of old with time on their hands.

Robyn stopped at a harbour restaurant for brunch, then toured all the historic landmarks: the Courthouse, the Baldwin House Museum where a medical missionary had lived with his family, the old Pioneer Inn—its bar-room decorated with original relics of the whaling days. At best it was something to do, something to fill in the day, before the ordeal which lay ahead of her.

She drifted along the harbour front and impulsively booked a Sunset Dinner sail on a three-masted schooner which left the harbour at five-thirty and was scheduled to return two hours later.

Robyn quite enjoyed it in a detached sort of way. They sailed along the West Maui shoreline and the trade winds were pleasantly mild. She ate *teriyaki* chicken and drank a considerable number of tropical cocktails while she watched the entertainment. For a girl who drank rarely, she was doing very well, particularly when the dancing girls made such a sexual impact with their sensuous movements: the Hawaiian *hula* to its gentle swaying music and the Tahitian *tamure* with its more primitive drum-beats.

Having induced a hazy mellowness with all the drinks she had consumed, Robyn wished they could just keep on sailing, but they docked precisely at seven-thirty, and by eight she was back at the hotel.

The bed was already turned down; another flower placed on the top sheet. The petals of the frangipani lei on the coffee-table had turned brown. Robyn picked it up and dropped it into the disposal bin. Her thoughts about the consummation of her marriage were too disturbing to allow herself to dwell on them.

Yet if she was strictly honest with herself—which was difficult—she wanted to feel the same thing again! And it had to be Julian who had made love to her! If it was David...then in some inexplicable way they were one and the same person. Which was a mad thought, but mad thoughts were quite familiar to her now. She was almost at home with them.

She wandered into the dressing-room and stared at her reflection in the wall-mirror behind the vanity-table. That stranger is me, she thought... that person who wants a man so much she'd do anything for him.

Had her mother felt like that? Her sisters? All these years she had been standing back and judging them as foolishly dependent on men, and she hadn't known, hadn't realised what it could mean to them, or to herself. She would be kinder in future, less critical and more understanding.

An hour later she was in bed, waiting in the darkness. The tension of last night was gone. So many things were now resolved in her heart, if not in her mind. She was in love with Julian Lassiter. Whether it was David or not who made love to her, all she had to do was believe it was Julian and the experience was sublime. Julian was as necessary to her life as air and water. Maybe more so.

She remembered the things he had told her that first night at Swan Court. Davey had come to Maui for a last taste of all that was most pleasurable in this world, and Julian was prepared to go along with his brother's wishes, regardless of his own.

Tonight she would make it pleasurable for him, whoever he was, because either way it was what Julian wanted. So she couldn't do wrong. It was Julian she was pleasing, fulfilling Julian's needs; only Julian.

The door clicked open and shut. Robyn's pulse-rate crashed into overdrive, but not through fear. She felt rather than saw the mass of the man in the darkness. He stood by the bed and she could sense his tension. She hitched herself up and reached out her hand to his. Strong, supple fingers curled around hers and gripped hard.

'I've worried about you all day,' he said huskily, his voice matted with concern.

'Love me,' Robyn breathed, her need shaking through the bare whisper. Her eyes probed the darkness for his in mute pleading. 'Love me just a little.'

A guttural sound of anguish broke from his throat and he reached for her, his hands finding her body and drawing her out of the bed, his arms cradling her tightly, possessively, crushing her to him as he lifted her, then holding her fast to the hard strength of his body as he let her legs swing down to stand on her own two feet.

Violent kisses showered her face, punctuated with inarticulate murmurings that throbbed with love and need and want beyond bearing. His lips seared a trail down the tender flesh of her throat. The breath was painfully expunged from her lungs as his arms mercilessly imprinted her body on his, hands urgently moulding her soft curves to his sexual need.

And without thought, acting on sheer animal instinct, she exulted in the hard core of his virility, grinding her softness around it. His whole body tensed, arched into her, his head thrown back as a groan of savage pleasure erupted from his throat. Robyn lifted her arms around his neck to draw him back to her, and the more pointed pressure of her full breasts on the taut muscles of his chest made him gasp, choking the groan into a cry of desperate want. His head snapped back. His mouth crashed on to hers, insatiable in plundering all she offered him.

His hand curved under her buttocks, lifting, squeezing the pliant flesh to an even more intimate awareness of his arousal with compelling sexuality. 'Now,' he growled, the word rasping on a harsh breath, hardly distinguishable, but he swung her with him, half carrying her the step that took them to the edge of the bed.

'No! Wait! Wait!' she cried, panting with her own fevered arousal. Under other circumstances she would have let him have his way, given in to anything; but something, intuition, a panicky sixth sense, told her that this night should be savoured as no other night in her life. She wanted all of him, not as it had been last night.

Her urgent plea stopped him, but she felt the massive rise and fall of his chest as he fought for restraint. Her own breathing was rapid and shallow. She felt light-headed, and her stomach and thighs started to shake uncontrollably as she wriggled down from his hold and pushed her feet on to the carpet.

Her hands dropped quickly, sliding over the silk fabric of his shirt to find the top button. An unnatural stillness descended on the man whose arms had convulsively locked their bodies together again. It was as if the whole life force of him was standing in suspended judgement. He had stopped breathing. Only his heart beat on.

Robyn forced the button through the hole with trembling fingers that refused to co-operate in making it a simple task. Her hand traced down the line of his chest to the next one which resisted her efforts to release it for long, frustrating seconds. His flesh tremored violently under her panicky fumbling, and with a choked-off explosion of sound he erupted into action, tearing her away from him and laying her across the bed.

She heard the sound of popping buttons as he ripped the shirt from his body and tossed it away; then the drag of cloth as he threw his trousers down. His arms burrowed under her waist, pulling her towards him, lifting, and with a wild cry of exultation, he drove deeply into her.

The shock of it jack-knifed Robyn's body for a moment, but the after-shock was a tidal wave of mind-clenching sensation that swept all thought into useless flotsam. If there was any conscious surrender to what was happening, Robyn didn't know of it. Her whole being was focused entirely on the relentless surging inside her...mindless, mindless, mindless, terrible, wanton and mindless...and any salvaging of self was beyond consideration. She belonged to him, was owned by him, and her body exulted in every thrust that commanded her submission.

She felt the warmth of his coming, but it seemed to make no difference to his need for her. He went on, plundering with an animal greed that knew no tomorrow, as if there were only this night and he must take all she would give, glory in it, savour it, lose himself in it.

His rapacious need sent Robyn into a world she had never known before, where every sensation that is not pleasure becomes pain, and all pain is pleasure. She was beyond all cohesion, beyond all thought, responding to a primitive mating that was beyond her capacity to control. She had no idea whether she lived through aeons or through seconds. How long was time? She had no understanding of it, no need to know.

He gathered her body to his. They intertwined, and sought to know and feel and experience all that they were with a passionate greed that knew no satiation. And Robyn learnt that lovemaking never ended, even when it was finished. Her body was such a seething mass of sensation that even the lightest of kisses could make her erupt into a sea of bliss and contentment.

Perhaps she slept, or maybe there was a time when she was only semi-conscious. She laid his head on the soft cushion of her breasts and his breathing was hard and strained like a long-distance runner. Her hand stroked the strong curve of his back. Her thigh brushed his in languorous pleasure. He kissed her as though her flesh were the sweetest honey.

She wanted it to go on, never to stop. She saw the faint glow of the rising sun start to illuminate the edge of the curtain. Her arms folded around him to hold him to her more securely, for ever and for ever. All she had to do was stay awake another ten or fifteen minutes and she could look down and see who the man was who had given her this night of nights.

As if he had read her thoughts he stirred, started to move away.

'Don't go!' She tried to restrain him.

'The conditions...' His voice was harsh and unnatural.

'They don't matter any more,' she insisted, pressing her lips once more to his.

He kissed her long and hard, then put her away from him. 'I'm afraid they do,' he said on a rasping breath.

And, while Robyn's senses were still swimming from his farewell kiss, he swiftly pulled on his clothes and made his departure.

Why did he have to go? Robyn thought, miserable with the cold loneliness of separation. She had made the conditions. Surely she could be allowed to unmake them? It hurt that he could detach himself from the intimacy they had shared, no matter what had been agreed upon.

Robyn knew all about detachment. She had been practising it all her life. It was the best protection against being hurt. But what hurt was he expecting her to inflict? She hadn't held back any part of herself. Why should he?

Unless the conditions suited him too well to break!

Was it Julian, playing out some hideous deception?

Or was it David, the intellectual, analytic scientist who could not afford to become emotionally involved when he had already offered the rest of his life to medical research?

Robyn decided that the question had to be resolved once and for all, or she really would go mad thinking about it. And there was one sure way of finding out. When the man entered her room tonight he would be given no chance of hiding his identity. She would switch on the light. And everything that was happening to her would be revealed.

If it was David, she would have to accept that there were some things in life that were totally inexplicable.

If it was Julian, no matter that her heart sang at the thought, he had a lot of explaining to do.

And there was one last consideration that filled her with fear. Her instincts clamoured out that whatever the result was going to be, she was opening up a Pandora's box of immeasurable troubles, and her life would be altered for ever after.

CHAPTER NINE

ROBYN stayed around the hotel the next day. She wanted, hoped for, feared a chance meeting with Julian or David or both of the Lassiter brothers. She needed to know, yet she did not know how she would cope with the knowledge if her lover proved to be David.

She didn't love David. She didn't even know him. She didn't want to know him if he was going to die and leave her alone for ever. How could she bear it? To be given a taste of what a relationship could be like, and have it torn away from her; it was too cruel.

And it was wrong. She didn't believe, couldn't believe that it was possible to respond like that to someone she hadn't responded to at all in their few brief encounters.

She didn't know why or how, but it had to be Julian. Perhaps David had discovered at the last minute that he was too sick, incapable of going through with it, and Julian had taken his place because David had wanted him to have a child, any child to carry on the Lassiter name.

She remembered David's delight when he thought she had come to Maui with Julian. Hope for the future, he had said. And with Julian so anti-women and anti-marriage, he was unlikely ever to have children in the normal course of things. But if David had pressured him, Julian would do anything for his brother, anything! He was entirely ruthless for someone he loved!

But it had worried him. He had cared about her feelings. Maybe he was coming to love her as she loved him. The thought made Robyn feel almost deliriously happy. But he had to tell her the truth now. She would forgive him the deception. Forgive him anything, as long as he would love her as he had done the last two nights.

It had to be Julian. Had to be...

Robyn was tempted to call him, ask to see him, but she didn't want him to deny the truth, and without any surprise element in their meeting she was sure he would be in absolute control of himself and the situation. There would be no tell-tale reaction to her unless he was caught unprepared. And David had the same iron will. Neither man was likely to reveal anything that might compromise their position.

The best way of attacking the problem was to wait until tonight, and, with that decision made, Robyn waited for the appointed hour with fretting impatience.

Doubts kept worming into her mind. What if it was David, and not Julian? She kept shying away from the terrible thought. She was even tempted to keep to the conditions she had made. Her need for a repetition of last night's experience was close to shameless, and once he took her in his arms again she would be lost to any other consideration. She knew she would. And then he would leave her in the darkness and she would be none the wiser.

It wouldn't do. She had to regain some control over what was happening to her, even if it meant more heartache and mental anguish. She couldn't keep living with this kind of emotional chaos.

At five minutes to ten she switched off all the lights and sat on the side of the bed nearest the hallway. The reading-lamp was only an arm's stretch away. She had wrapped the *yukata* around her, all too conscious of the vulnerability of her nakedness beneath it, but at least she was decently covered for the moment of truth.

Nervous apprehension sent uncontrollable tremors through her body. She wrapped her arms around her chest, holding on tight to her resolution. Besides, it wouldn't be David. It had to be Julian. And she would work it all out with him . . . somehow.

The door clicked open. Her heart thundered in her ears. She forced herself to wait until the door clicked shut, then leapt to her feet. She snapped on the bedside-lamp, and took the fateful step that would let her identify her visitor beyond question.

His back was turned to her, his hand still upon the door, but even in the dim light of the lamp there was no mistaking the blackness of his hair. The relief that surged through Robyn was dizzying.

Julian . . . Julian . . . her heart sang the name with a joy that knew no bounds.

He turned slowly, his face still in shadow, but unmistakably Julian's face. The deep-set eyes were hooded. The distinctive planes of cheek and jawline seemed even more definitively drawn in the soft play of light. The taut column of his throat was laid bare by an open-necked shirt that was already half unbuttoned. Its silky fabric was white, like the buttons Robyn had picked up from the floor this morning.

For a long moment they stared at each other, neither moving nor speaking. Robyn felt as if she were poised on the edge of something too momentous to be hurried. What was said now would inevitably affect the rest of her life.

And Julian . . . his eyes were burning at her under those lowered lids. His throat moved, but the rest of him was still, unnaturally still, as if his whole being was concentrated on harnessing all his strength to his formidable will. He broke the tense silence with controlled deliberation.

'I hope I didn't startle you. I was about to call out to warn you it was me,' he said evenly, his voice revealing no surprise or shock at having his deception uncovered. 'Davey asked me to come down and explain that he cannot come tonight. And to give you back your room-key. He...'

'No!' The protest burst from her throat, as sharp as the pain that sliced through her at his calm denial of what had seemed so self-evident. Her hands flew up to her throat which had tightened over the horrible possibility that Julian was not lying.

He stepped towards her, his hands opening in apologetic appeal. 'I'm sorry. I probably should have knocked, but I wasn't sure you'd answer the door, under the circumstances.'

Robyn's mind clutched at other possibilities. Julian was making excuses for his presence. Covering up. Protecting himself and his brother.

'The fact is,' he continued, the black eyebrows lowering in concern, 'Davey is too ill to keep the agreed arrangement, and he leaves for Sydney tomorrow. He's going back to the medical centre at the university.'

'No,' she whispered, stepping back from him and shaking her head in agonised denial. It couldn't have been David. She wouldn't believe it. She couldn't. Every instinct cried out in revolt, every atom of her being heaved a rebellion against accepting Julian's bare-faced lie. It had to be a lie!

'I'm afraid so,' he said gravely. 'It's impossible for him to carry on.' His hands made a helpless gesture and his voice dropped to a note of soft finality. 'There is no more that can be done, Robyn. There either is a child, or there isn't. He is...not capable...of coming to you again.'

The blood drained from Robyn's face as her head reeled with what he was saying, trying to take it in, to match it with what she knew was true: the man's harsh breathing on her breasts last night, and David exhausted, unable to carry on.

And Julian, always so controlled, a cynical, self-confessed woman-hater—would he have been capable of the passion that had poured from her lover of last night? Yet, if it had been David, it seemed too incredible to be true.

Her intuition fought against accepting it, shrieking with frantic persistence that it couldn't be true. But it had to be so.

She felt that her whole life-force was being punched out of her body. And pain, pain such as she had never known before, flooded through all the empty spaces and engulfed her. She turned blindly, half tottered to the sofa, and collapsed on it in a crumpled heap, her back hunched in instinctive defence against the presence of the man who had shattered her existence.

'Robyn...'

The cry jangled in her ears, increasing her terrible anguish. Julian's voice, David's voice; so indistinguishable; nothing made sense to her, nothing!

A hand closed gently over her shoulder, just as it had done...her mind screamed at its duplicity and she wrenched herself free from that insidious touch. Her head snapped up and her eyes blazed at Julian Lassiter with a fierce rejection, hating him for not being the man he should have been.

'Don't ever...ever...touch me again!' she cried hoarsely, each word scourging him with the intensity of her pain. 'You enter my room...invade my privacy...as if it was no consideration at all. You pass my key around as if I were some paid servant whose feelings don't matter. And since your brother doesn't require my body for any more service...'

'Robyn, no!' His face whitened, contorted with sorrow. 'It isn't like that!'

'Don't you tell me what it's like!' she hissed through clenched teeth. 'I'm the one who feels humiliated and...and soiled.'

'No...' he groaned, and twisted away from her, pacing in agitation to the bed then wheeling back and striding jerkily past the coffee-table. He swept the curtains aside, pulled the glass door open, and stepped out on to the balcony. He leaned on the railing, hands gripping hard, and his shoulders hunched over.

Robyn hated him, hated herself, hated with a savage hatred that burned into more pain. She had done it for him, given herself to him, and he didn't even know it. And the man who had shared every possible intimacy with her was his brother, his brother who had done...who had given her all that he was.

Tears swam into her eyes and rolled unheeded down her cheeks. David had given so much that he was ill from it, and it was over. Everything was over. How could she ever have Julian now, when she would remember, always remember the last night with David?

Aloha! Goodbye to everything, she thought despairingly.

Julian turned around from the balcony railing and stepped back in the room, sliding the door shut behind him. Robyn closed her eyes. She couldn't bear to look at him and she had to stem the well of tears somehow.

'I'm sorry,' he said, and for once his voice wasn't controlled or even steady. It shook with deep, riveting anxiety. 'I never imagined it would be...could be...such a painful ordeal for you. It was Davey's last desire. I couldn't...I just couldn't smash it, Robyn.'

He made some guttural sound and continued in hoarse, driven tones. 'It was the only way, but I didn't know, I miscalculated. The means to an end...can't always be fully assessed beforehand. And now...now it's too late to change anything.'

She didn't want his sympathy or his guilt. It only increased her inner agony. She wished he would go and leave her alone, but couldn't find the control to speak even those words. The lump in her throat was impassable and the tears wouldn't stop. They kept swimming into her eyes and squeezing through her lashes.

She heard him draw out one of the chairs by the small dining-table and settle heavily on to it. 'What do you want to do, Robyn?' he asked. 'What do you want done? I hate to see your pain!' he added on a desperate note of pleading.

She shook her head and had to bite her lips to hold in the sobs that threatened to break from the lump in her throat.

'You seemed so hard-headed that first night at Swan Court,' he remarked despairingly. 'An experienced woman of the world in every sense. I was staggered, moved, when you made what was obviously an emotional decision. But then your conditions...no involvement. I thought you were rationalising everything, that you really wanted a child of your own and this was as good an opportunity as any.'

He muttered an inarticulate imprecation that suggested self-disgust. 'I can see now you've been hurt in a way that I never envisaged, was too blind to comprehend. And I regret it, very deeply.' He sighed again, and his voice softened. 'For what you've done, for what you've tried to do, Robyn, ask anything of me at all, anything you want.'

'I want you to go,' she sobbed, unable to bear any more.

The greatest sadness, the old lady had said. And how right, how very right she had been.

It wasn't Julian's fault that she had chosen to do what he had asked. She shouldn't blame him, or hate him for not fulfilling her self-deluding dreams. Nor could she hate David for what he had done. But there was nothing left for her.

And, while the old lady had been right about some things, she had been wrong about Julian. No matter how much her heart and mind cried out for him, they could never marry now. His brother would always lie between them, a memory that could never be expunged.

She lifted bleak, tear-washed eyes to the man she could never have and forced herself to say what had to be said. 'I want you to go away. To go away with David. And I don't want to see either of you, ever again. It would be...intolerable.'

He bowed his head, rubbed his hand over his eyes for several agonising moments, then pushed himself out of the chair, and slowly straightened to his full height. 'Yes, you're right,' he muttered. 'It is...intolerable.'

His face was all harsh planes, more austere than she had ever seen it, and, when he lifted his gaze to meet hers, the haunted look in his eyes seemed to reflect her own inner agony.

'I won't ever intrude on your privacy again,' he assured her softly. 'It won't mean anything to you, but you've changed my feelings about women for ever. It was...a privilege...to know you, for however short a time. I hope...' He closed his eyes and shook his head. *'Aloha,'* he whispered huskily, and strode quickly away.

He jerked to a halt by the bedside-table, placed her room-key on it, then walked even more swiftly to the door. He did not look back at her.

'Aloha,' she whispered as the door shut behind him. And the tears started rolling again, tears of grief for what might have been, because Julian had come to care for her; and it was too late.

CHAPTER TEN

ROBYN didn't know how long she sat on the sofa after Julian left. Her mind was a haze of pain, her body an ache of emptiness, and the loneliness of utter despair was a pall from which there was no escape. She didn't remember going to bed or falling asleep, but when she woke the next morning she felt no differently. A few hours had been blanked out. That was all.

She took herself out to the sun, but nothing could brighten her spirits or lighten the darkness in her soul. She lay by the pool, mechanically working on getting a tan. After all, she was supposed to show something for her Hawaiian holiday.

The beeper on her telephone was signalling a message when she returned to her room. She rang the hotel concierge who informed her that there was a letter for her at the desk. She went up to the lobby to collect it, not even pausing to consider who might have written to her.

But it was not really a letter; only a sealed envelope with her name and room number scrawled across it. In Julian's handwriting!

She told herself to throw it away unopened, that it would only sharpen the pain that had simmered down to a tolerable level, but her fingers played traitor to her will, tearing through the flap even as her tired mind listlessly argued the point.

It contained one sheet of notepaper and a business card for the Lassiter Corporation. On the back of the card were printed two telephone numbers—one business; one personal. The message on the notepaper was short.

Robyn—
    If you are ever in need of anything—any help or assistance—at any time, for anything at all, I will always be available. Just call me. Julian.

Like a good big brother, she thought, remembering with savage irony that the same brotherliness he extended to David was precisely what she had wanted from Julian...until she had learnt better. And that bitter lesson was unlikely to be forgotten, ever. She would never be able to see him without pain, and Robyn had already experienced enough of that without inviting more.

Nevertheless, she kept the card and the note. It was all she had left of him. The lei was gone. He was gone. And it was some small comfort to have something to show he had cared.

The rings on her left hand didn't count. They were the reminders of her marriage to David. And she only kept them because a child might have been conceived on one of those two nights.

Biologically it was possible, even probable, since she had been right in the middle of her fertile cycle, but Robyn had known couples where conception hadn't happened straight away. Sometimes they tried for months before achieving the desired result. Nature could be very capricious. She hoped it would be with her. It would avoid so many complications.

But Robyn could not ignore the possibility, however ambivalent her feelings were towards it. Somewhere in her life she still wanted a child of her own, and there were moments of painful compassion when she still

wanted David to have his child; but she was not sure
how she would cope with such an eventuality.

Robyn told herself she would face that when it came,
if it came. Meanwhile she had to get through the days
as best she could.

Life flowed around her during the rest of her stay on
Maui, but Robyn did not feel part of it. It was like an
insubstantial dream. She couldn't recapture her sense of
pleasure in her beautiful surroundings. She wanted to
go home. Only the ingrained principle of taking what
she had paid for kept her at the hotel until the designated end of her holiday.

It was with almost overwhelming relief that Robyn
packed her bags and caught the shuttle back to Maui
Airport. Nevertheless, as she walked up to the entrance
of the airport terminal a haunting shiver ran down her
spine. The old lady was not there, but Robyn's memory
was all too acute—replaying the scene of a week ago,
even to the exact words spoken. It was impossible to
prevent herself from turning around and looking at the
spot where she had first seen Julian Lassiter.

It took all Robyn's will-power to recollect herself and
keep going. She checked in for her flight and had her
suitcase directed through to Sydney. Fortunately she did
not have to wait long before boarding the Hawaiian
Airways plane. It was a much longer wait for the Qantas
connecting flight at Honolulu, but the terminal there held
no poignant memories, and home was closer.

The last leg of the flight took ten hours. With her
limited capacity and experience, a few solid drinks helped
put Robyn to sleep and the night passed without much
stress at all. It was early morning before she was roused
to full consciousness with the pilot's announcement of
their approach to Mascot Airport.

Robyn stirred from her fitful dozing and looked out of the porthole window. They were flying over the lakes of the Central Coast, just north of Sydney; the beautiful waterways marking their unique and distinctive pattern on the land below; the impressive fjords of the Hawkesbury River winding their convoluted way inland from the sea; and then the harbour gracing the city with its myriad inlets and coves. Surely this had to be one of the most beautiful scenes in the world.

The great coathanger bridge hung majestically across the misty water and sunshine bounced off the white sails of the Opera House roof. Their familiar lines made them all the more dear to her, and Robyn felt a strong tug of love for her own country. It was good to be home.

It was even better, an hour or so later, to walk into her small terraced house at Paddington and close the rest of the world out. She unpacked immediately, needing to have everything back to normal as soon as possible. Somehow she had to pick up the threads of her old life and weave them into a workable pattern that would blanket the pain; familiar routines, work, keeping up business contacts, concentrating hard on new travel concepts.

She did not remember her resolution about being more sympathetic in her judgements until her mother telephoned a few days later, asking about her holiday in Hawaii and bringing her up to date with the current family news.

The lives of her sisters seemed to be flowing smoothly for once, and her mother had found a new partner for bridge at the senior citizens' club.

'And he doesn't mind at all that I use my intuition to bid my cards,' her mother said with warm pleasure. 'In fact, he seems to appreciate it.'

He, Robyn thought with a touch of her old cynicism, then swiftly corrected herself. Why shouldn't her mother find pleasure in another man's companionship? It had been three years since she had found the courage to divorce that awful George, and Robyn now understood the kind of loneliness her mother suffered between husbands.

'He sounds nice, Mum,' she remarked kindly, and her mother sounded surprised and pleased by the comment.

'Yes. Yes, he is, Robyn. A real gentleman.' Then, with a wistful hope in her voice, she asked, 'Did you meet anyone nice on your holiday?'

It was a tactful hope that Robyn had replaced Larry with someone else. Ironically enough, Larry was so far in the past, it seemed a life ago. But it was most unlikely that Marjorie Kent would understand or approve of what her youngest daughter had done.

Robyn looked down at the rings on her left hand and prevaricated. 'Yes, I did, Mum. I'll let you know if anything comes of it.'

Like a child.

And only then would she ever tell her mother about her marriage to David Lassiter. But at least the ground had been laid if the telling became necessary.

'Is he an Australian?' her mother asked, eager for more information and all too obvious in her desire to see her wayward daughter matched up with someone.

'Yes, Mum. From Sydney as well,' Robyn sighed, and turned the conversation back to the obliging bridge-player who gallantly didn't mind her mother's fickle handling of rules when it came to bidding cards.

As usual, it was an easy matter to re-involve her mother in her own affairs, and the call ended on a cheerful note.

Robyn considered calling her sisters, but didn't feel she could cope with any more enquiries about her holiday. In a few weeks, if she wasn't pregnant, then she would make the effort really to communicate with both Jodie and Barbara.

It was wrong—what she had done—cutting herself off from them. They were her family, and, however little they seemed to have in common with her, surely some bond remained; a bond that could come to mean something. As it so obviously did with the Lassiters.

Robyn winced at the memory and tried to settle back to work. She was trying to form a new concept using archaeology in Portugal and Spain, but couldn't concentrate long enough to gather the right ideas together. When the doorbell heralded a visitor, she pushed her notes away with a feeling of relief. Any distraction from her inner turmoil was welcome.

Robyn had turned the front room of her narrow little house into her place of business. It was not at all unusual for travel agents to call on her, so she had no sense of premonition about answering the door.

The woman standing on the tiny front porch had a cold, imperious air. She was tall, expensively dressed in a green woollen suit and a beige silk blouse adorned with ropes of pearls. Her strong-boned face carried her age well, although Robyn guessed she was in her sixties. Her silver-blonde hair was elegantly coiffured into a French roll; her pale blue eyes were as hard as ice; and her whole expression was distinctly haughty as she surveyed Robyn from head to toe.

'Miss Robyn Walker?' she asked, as if the name were acid on her tongue.

'That's right.' Robyn switched on a politely enquiring smile. 'Can I help you?'

'I am Janet Lassiter. David's mother,' the woman said with frigid pride. 'And I've come to talk to you.'

The abrupt and unexpected introduction left Robyn floundering in a sea of uncertainties again. Her first impulse was to turn the woman away. Janet Lassiter exuded a barely repressed hostility, and all Robyn's defensive instincts cried out for her to shut the door on any more pain the Lassiter family might bring her. But pride forbade it. Pride insisted that she meet any challenge this woman threw at her. And answer it.

'Please come in,' she invited, the words slipping out before she could reconsider, before she remembered that pride had prodded her into accepting Julian's and David's company that first night at Swan Court.

Janet Lassiter stepped inside. Robyn waved an invitation for her to enter the small sitting-room that adjoined the office. The woman walked stiffly to the far end of the room, her gaze sweeping around critically as she took up a position in front of the gas-fire which was not lit.

Robyn felt all too conscious of what the woman saw— the old second-hand furniture which was solid and serviceable, but hardly in the antique class. Robyn had brightened up the two-seater sofa and armchairs with gay cushions, picking up the colours of the travel posters that decorated the white-painted walls. The effect was cheerful and cosy, but the class of great wealth was certainly missing.

'Would you like to sit down?' Robyn offered stiffly.

The woman did not move. She eyed Robyn for several more tense moments, her mouth thinning in disapproval at the casual attire of sweater and slacks. Robyn folded her arms and waited, refusing to be intimidated. Her clothes were perfectly respectable and she had nothing to be ashamed of. Absolutely nothing!

'What I have to say won't take long,' Janet Lassiter finally replied, her chin lifting in disdain of any hospitality Robyn might offer. 'Even though it was my son's decision, I can't approve of what he did. For you to take advantage of his illness shows exactly what type of person you are.'

'Take advantage?' Robyn echoed disbelievingly.

'Men can be incredibly stupid over a pretty face,' Janet bit out scathingly. 'I thought Julian was smart enough not to make the same mistake twice. Just because you've fooled him, don't think I'm going to stand by and see you collect Davey's inheritance. I'll fight you every inch of the way. Even if you have a child.' Her face contorted with revulsion. 'How you could do it . . . how you could play on my son's . . .'

'I didn't do the playing,' Robyn retorted fiercely. The implication that she was a fortune-hunter was unendurable. 'It was your son who played on my sympathies. Let me tell you, Mrs Lassiter, if I had the choice over again, I'd run a thousand miles before submitting to your son's desire to have a child.'

Red patches burnt across the older woman's cheekbones. 'It was an aberration of the moment! In his right mind, Davey would never have thought of doing such a thing. To put himself in the hands of someone like you...'

'He's not in my hands!' Robyn shot back in furious resentment. Her arms snapped out to make a vehement gesture of dismissal. 'You can keep your Lassiter name, and all your precious money! All I want is for every one of you high-and-mighty Lassiters to stay out of my life!'

The icy blue eyes narrowed. 'That's what you say now. Don't think I'm fool enough to trust you.'

'Then send me some legal waiver, and believe me, Mrs Lassiter, I'll sign it,' Robyn seethed at her. 'I'll be happy to be rid of all claim the Lassiter family could possibly have on me. And if I do have a child, that child will be mine. All mine! And nothing would suit me better.'

'I'll do that, Miss Walker, and then we'll prove just how far your word can be trusted,' Janet Lassiter declared triumphantly.

'I'll speed you on your way,' Robyn snapped, barely able to control the emotion churning through her. She gave vent to some of it by striding to the front door and opening it with noisy ceremony. Then, drawing on her last reserves of pride and dignity, she delivered her own ultimatum, her eyes raking the woman with bitter contempt as she made her haughty approach to the opened doorway.

'I don't want to see you again, Mrs Lassiter. I don't want to have contact with any Lassiter. I repeat—*any Lassiter*! I don't like what they are. I don't like what they do. Don't any one of you ever call on me again, for any reason!'

The woman hesitated in her step, pained uncertainty discomposing her face for a moment, then she swept past with regathered scorn. Robyn was already closing the door when Janet Lassiter paused again and turned back, her eyes glittering with accusation.

'How could you do it? My son is dying, and you don't care, do you? You went after what you wanted and you don't care at all.'

'I cared, Mrs Lassiter,' Robyn threw back at her, the pain and confusion of those two nights searing her heart. 'You will never know how much! And not all the wealth in the world would repay me for what I've given up for your son. I've paid, and am still paying, and will pay for the rest of my life, because I cared too much.'

And, trembling with the tortured force of her emotions, Robyn slammed the door in the other woman's face. She barely tottered back into the sitting-room before bursting into tears at the terrible injustice of Janet Lassiter's accusations.

The rest of the day passed in an agonised blur. Eventually she sat back down at her desk, but she didn't open any books or write any notes. When the doorbell rang again, she noticed that the room was dark. She didn't know how long she had been sitting there, didn't know what time it was, and didn't care. Whoever was at the door could go away.

But the caller was doggedly persistent. Even though there were no lights on in the house, he or she was not discouraged. The bell kept ringing with monotonous regularity until Robyn couldn't stand it any longer. She snapped on the desk-light, pushed herself to her feet, and walked listlessly to the front door, switching on the hallway light and porch light as a matter of course.

She should have looked through the peephole in the door. Normally she would have. But she wasn't thinking straight. Irritation with the intrusive bell-ringer drove her hand to the door-knob and she yanked open the door without any sense of caution.

It was a terrible mistake.

The man's face was grey; the austere lines more deeply carved; the eyes darkly haunted but burning at her with painful intensity. He looked as if he had aged ten years since she had last seen him, but there was no doubting who he was. There could only be one Julian Lassiter.

CHAPTER ELEVEN

THE impact of seeing him again was like absorbing a physical blow. Robyn's head swam, her stomach contracted, her legs turned to water, and she clutched on to the door for support.

'Robyn.' Her name was a harsh rasp of relief. His eyes raked her face with piercing concern. 'I was so worried when you didn't answer the door...you look ill!'

'What do you want, Julian?' she cried in bitter desperation. 'Why can't you and your family leave me alone? You agreed...'

'Janet told my father what she had done,' he explained quickly, his eyes anxiously pleading for her forbearance. 'I had to come and put it right. She's completely unbalanced with grief over Davey, Robyn. You mustn't take any notice of what she said to you today. Tomorrow she'll be begging your forgiveness. I swear to you...'

'Don't!' she begged, shaking her head in agonised protest. 'I don't want your promises. I don't want anything more to do with any of you. All you and your family have brought me since we first met is anguish and torment and pain. I want you to go away. Go away and leave me alone to get on with my life!'

He caught the door with a swiftly upraised arm as she tried to swing it shut. 'Robyn, please, we owe you...'

'Nothing!' she croaked, her throat raw with torn emotions.

'If there's a child...'

'It's mine! Mine! I won't take anything from you!'

'For God's sake...'

'No,' she sobbed, pushing frantically against the door.

'Robyn, listen to me.'

'I listened. You promised to leave me alone.'

'How can I leave you alone like this?' he cried despairingly. 'At least let me call someone to come and be with you. Your mother, someone...'

'I don't want anyone. Just go, Julian,' she pleaded, tortured beyond reason. 'You have no right to break into my home. No right to anything!'

His face contorted with raging conflicts. 'All right. But promise me, promise me you'll look after yourself, Robyn.'

'Yes!' She would have promised anything to be free of his tormenting presence.

He drew in a deep breath, his eyes scouring hers with urgent intensity. 'Be assured, there'll be no repetition of such appalling behaviour. I know that's no compensation for what has happened. But it will certainly never happen again.'

He dropped his arm from the door and it automatically slammed shut from her leaning force. Robyn sagged against it, shuddering from reaction. She heard the iron gate of her front porch clang shut and knew he was going away...again...and her heart drummed a mournful refrain.

But what else could she have done? Her love for Julian was hopeless, utterly hopeless! No good could ever come of seeing him again. Her marriage to David was obviously tearing his family apart. Even if she didn't have a child, they could never meet without remembering what had been planned, and done. And if she did have a child . . .

Robyn prayed that she wouldn't, that the grief of her association with the Lassiters could be put behind her some time in the future, not drawn into a lifetime of being continually reminded.

But as the days slowly passed by and the anxiously awaited proof that she was not pregnant did not come, Robyn felt more and more crushed by a sense of inevitability. When the time had gone beyond any feasible excuse, she took a pregnancy test.

An hour later, the small brown ring in the bottom of the test-tube was conclusive. However difficult it was to accept—and Robyn stared at it for a long time, hardly able to believe it—the result was positive. She was carrying David Lassiter's child, and decisions had to be made.

Robyn felt oddly numb, as if she were in a state of suspended animation while her life was being reshaped to admit the reality of a child, and all the repercussions that would come from it.

She took out the card that Julian had left for her at the concierge's desk in Maui and fingered it for a long time, agonising over the call that her conscience insisted should be made. David had the right to know that he had fathered a child.

But would Julian continue to leave her alone once he knew she was carrying David's one and only heir? The only Lassiter heir, since Julian himself had no children!

He would come. She knew he would. He would come, wanting to look after her and the child, and she could never find the strength to turn him away again. She knew she couldn't.

It was her baby, she argued frantically to herself. She could manage quite well without the Lassiters' help. All she had to do was prove to Julian that she didn't need what he had promised and he would go away. He would have no arguable reason for not doing so. Except, in her heart of hearts, she knew he had.

She thrust his card back into the drawer of her desk and reached for the telephone. Robyn couldn't remember the last time she had asked her mother for support, and it was difficult to do it now, but she was desperate to armour herself against Julian and the Lassiter family. She breathed a shaky sigh of relief when her mother answered her call.

'It's Robyn, Mum,' she said in a voice so weak and wobbly she hardly recognised it as her own.

'Oh! You've just caught me, dear. I was on my way out and...'

'Mum.' Robyn swallowed hard, hating the necessity to plead. 'Mum, I need to see you.'

There was a slight pause, then in a voice that was remarkably unlike her mother's, uncertain but with a slight thread of hope to it, 'Robyn, I'll come over straight away.'

The call was disconnected before Robyn could have second thoughts on the matter, but for the next half-hour she stewed over the coming meeting, swinging between the need to talk to someone sympathetic and fear that her mother would let her down once again. As long as Robyn could remember, her mother had been prone to ignoring or skating over the not-so-nice side of life. If she showed any disgust for what Robyn had done...

The doorbell rang, and when Robyn answered it her courage slipped even further. Marjorie Kent was a well-preserved woman in her early sixties; a woman who was very conscious of keeping up appearances; fashionably dressed and neatly groomed, with the kind of soft femininity that was attractive to men; a fluffy person, unequipped and disinclined to deal with hard realities.

'I'm sorry, Mum,' Robyn said distractedly. 'I didn't mean you to...'

'Robyn, please,' her mother broke in, her eyes projecting earnest appeal, 'don't pretend there's nothing wrong. It's been so long since you've asked me for anything. You never talk to me, not really. I want to help, if only you'll let me.'

Robyn frowned, remembering her own self-criticism about shutting her family out of her life. She looked hard at her mother and could not ignore the genuine sincerity that looked back at her. She took a deep breath and met her half-way.

'I'm not sure you will want to hear what I have to tell you, Mum, but since you've come, it might as well be done now.'

It was difficult to know where to start. Robyn saw her mother settled on the two-seater sofa in the sitting-room, but she shied away from directly facing the anxious enquiry in her mother's eyes. She stayed on her feet, wandering aimlessly around the room as she spoke, steeling herself to weather the shock and disapproval and try for some kind of understanding, if that was possible.

Marjorie Kent was shocked by what Robyn told her, but the shock drained into a pained sadness. Robyn finished explaining her position, and, when there was no barrage of questions or criticism, she dropped limply into the armchair opposite her mother and shot her a wary, defensive look, still anticipating a rejection of some kind.

Marjorie Kent shook her head. The large blue eyes that Robyn had inherited misted into watery greyness as she spoke, and, far from criticising, she talked in a tone of weary resignation. 'I'm not like you, Robyn. I couldn't do what you have done. I've always needed love in my life, someone who would love me, and whom I could love back. I haven't always made the right decisions.' Tears glittered on her lower lashes. 'I know they weren't right for you. I lost you somewhere, Robyn, failed you. The other girls were easier, but you were so many years younger and ... I just didn't cope very well with things.'

'I managed all right, Mum,' Robyn put in awkwardly, embarrassed and pained by the baring of her mother's feelings. She now understood the need for a man's love, and the defensive barriers she had built to protect herself against what she had seen as the fickleness of her mother's affection were being sorely tested.

'No.' Marjorie Kent shook her head sadly. 'You survived in your own way, Robyn. I hoped, I wanted different things for you, but we reap what we sow. I'm grateful that you've confided in me now. Whatever happens,' the tears rolled down her careworn cheeks, 'I am your mother, Robyn, and I'll stand by you as best I can.'

And suddenly the gulf that had existed between them for so long seemed to close. Robyn saw the aged weariness on her mother's face and was poignantly aware that everyone had only a certain allotted span and it was given to no one to live for ever. And this was her mother, her mother who had given life to her just as she would give life to the child inside her.

Robyn stumbled to her feet, tears streaming from her own eyes, and she rushed to her mother and hugged her, and they wept together, reforging the bond that had been missing for so many, many years.

'I understand your feelings about the Lassiters, Robyn,' her mother said eventually. 'But I think you should reconsider your decision to keep them out of your life. Because it's not just your life any more, my dear, and one day you will have to answer to your child for your decisions. And if the answer isn't adequate to him or to her...'

'I'm not judging you any more, Mum,' Robyn rushed out apologetically.

Marjorie Kent shook her head. 'Robyn, I know the mistakes I made. It's difficult to be all things to everyone, and most of us fail. What I'm saying is, it's a hard life alone, Robyn. And Julian Lassiter sounds like a good man. A fair man. I think your child would benefit from having an uncle who is willing to provide everything you won't be able to. You should think about that, Robyn.'

And Robyn did, long after her mother left. Of course, her mother didn't know of her love for Julian. Robyn hadn't told her that, couldn't bear to open up such a deep, private pain to anyone else, no matter how sympathetic the listener. But maybe, by the time she had the baby, the pain could be contained at a tolerable level. After all, she would have her very own child to love then. Her need for Julian's love would surely be lessened by the baby's coming.

Her mother was right. It wouldn't be fair to deprive her child of its birthright as David Lassiter's son or daughter. She would accept whatever Julian insisted that the child should have.

After its birth.

Until then she would lead her own life as best she could, keeping Julian and the Lassiter family at a very firm distance.

But one thing had to be done without any further delay. David had to be told. It was wrong to put off the ordeal of calling Julian when the news of her pregnancy would bring some joy to what little life David had left. And, after she had done it, her conscience would be completely clear.

With her future course firmly decided in her mind, Robyn once more withdrew Julian's card from her desk-drawer and dialled his business number before her sense of purpose could be eroded by doubts.

'The Lassiter Corporation,' a pleasantly feminine voice announced. 'How can I help you?'

For one strangled moment, Robyn's vocal cords were paralysed. Would Julian leave her alone, give her the time and space she needed, once he knew she was pregnant? What if he...

'Who's calling please?' came the polite prompt.

The urge to hang up was almost irresistible, but Robyn pushed back the panicky doubts and forced herself to reply. 'I want...I want to speak to Mr Julian Lassiter, if he's available.'

'I'll put you through to his personal secretary.'

Robyn waited with nervous impatience until she was connected, then repeated her request more aggressively. After all, Julian couldn't make her accept anything she didn't want.

'I'm afraid Mr Lassiter is in conference at the moment and is unavailable. Would you care to leave a message, Miss...?'

'Walker,' she answered automatically, while ambivalent feelings warred through her: regret and frustration that she wouldn't hear his voice, relief that she would be spared the anguish of listening to him and knowing he only cared for her as a brother might.

But at least her mind calmed down from its chaos and the pressure squeezing her heart lost some of its tight grip. She was able to form a message that was to the point but satisfactorily discreet.

'Would you please tell him . . . that what he wanted to happen . . . has happened.'

'What he wanted to happen . . . has happened,' the secretary repeated methodically.

Tears started into Robyn's eyes at the flat indifference in the woman's voice. The words meant nothing to her, yet they were words that carried the heavy import of an irrevocable change in Robyn's life.

'And the name again, Miss . . . ?'

'Walker. Robyn Walker.'

She was already lowering the receiver when the secretary's voice rose several decibels, the polite indifference replaced by almost hysterical anxiety.

'Oh, please! Please! Hold on to the line, Miss Walker! Don't hang up!'

'But . . .' Robyn started in protest, utterly bewildered by the desperate plea, only to be interrupted again, even more wildly.

'Miss Walker, I beg of you, there can't be any buts. My orders are very strict and Mr Lassiter is not a man to be disobeyed. A call from you has priority over everything else. No matter where he is or what he's doing. It will only take me a few moments to get Mr Lassiter for you, Miss Walker. Please, please, please don't go!'

Robyn was stunned into compliance for a moment. 'Always available', Julian had written on the notepaper, but it still astounded her that he had meant it to this extent. But then she remembered his ruthless efficiency; how he had arranged her marriage, arranged her life to fit the circumstances, always thinking ahead, calculating and being prepared for every possibility; and she realised that he would never have left a call from her to chance. Not when it might mean good news for David.

And what else did Julian have ready planned in case she was pregnant?

Robyn crashed the telephone receiver down on a wave of sheer panic. She didn't want to talk to him and suffer the torment of fighting his will when half of her wanted to give in to it. She had done what she had to do, given him the message to pass on to David. She couldn't allow Julian to take charge of her life. Not until she was ready to cope with him.

And it wasn't as if she was alone any more. She had her mother to turn to. She didn't need his help.

But would Julian recognise her right to be left alone now? The situation was different when he had come to her door after Janet Lassiter's visit. Then she had only been the woman who might be carrying David's child. What licence would he feel the confirmation of her pregnancy gave him?

One thing was certain. The response to her call put beyond a shadow of doubt that Julian had something planned. The only questions were, how long would it be before he put his plan into action, and how ruthless did he intend to be in carrying out his will? Robyn suspected that his consideration for her would come to a very quick end if it conflicted with his consideration for David's child.

CHAPTER TWELVE

JULIAN came the next morning.

He looked even worse than he had last time: white and strained, with shadows under his eyes as if he had spent a sleepless night wrestling with the problem of overriding her wishes. But the determination stamped upon his face warned Robyn that he would fight any opposition to his purpose, and he didn't waste any time with a greeting.

'It's gone too far now, Robyn,' he stated, his body displaying the tension of a steel trap poised to close on its victim. 'There is no turning back. We made an agreement, and while I understand why you feel about me the way you do, I have a responsibility to the child you're carrying, and the child comes first.'

He had no idea in the world how she felt about him, Robyn thought with savage irony. But that was beside the point. Better that he didn't or any future relationship between them—for the child's sake—would be impossible.

'Come in and tell me what you have in mind,' she invited, her eyes flashing him a spirited warning as she added, 'But that doesn't mean I'll go along with it, Julian.'

He was startled by even that show of ready acquiescence, and Robyn suddenly realised he had been expecting another outright rejection from her. However, he was quick to take advantage of her offer, stepping smartly inside and walking straight ahead to the sitting-room. He took up the same commanding position his stepmother had, but Robyn didn't remain standing this time.

She sank into the nearest armchair, needing to conserve her strength in every way she could because the turmoil inside her was frightening. To maintain her veneer of calm composure strained her control to the limit, and she was determined to be reasonable...if he was.

'You told David?' she asked, trying to pitch her voice at a matter-of-fact level.

When he didn't immediately answer, she flicked him a glance and found his eyes raking her face, sharply observant, anxiously probing, so intensely focused on her that Robyn felt she was being devoured by them and nothing could stay hidden from him.

'Of course,' he said softly. 'Davey is very grateful to you—delighted.'

She instantly dropped her lashes, but the burning memory of what had been done to accomplish her pregnancy brought a hot sweep of colour into her pale cheeks.

'So what do you want now, Julian?' she demanded flatly.

He winced and dropped his gaze for a moment. When he looked up his expression was more bleak than Robyn had ever seen it before. 'What I want is irrelevant. Whatever we feel about each other is unimportant. I'm thinking only of your welfare, Robyn. And the child's. I've brought someone with me. Someone to help you.'

'What do you mean, help me?' Robyn demanded suspiciously, her hackles rising at the idea of having some stranger thrust upon her.

'Let me explain,' Julian said quickly. 'Tina Stavlikos is from my personal staff, Robyn. In fact, she's one of the best assistants I've ever had. She can do anything she has to, and I'm sure she can be a great help to you in your business.'

'I don't need any help with my business,' Robyn flared at him.

'Then she can do whatever services you might require of her,' Julian returned with steely purpose. 'If nothing else, she can be company for you. And it also means you will not have to deal directly with me.'

He was putting a watch-dog on her. That was what he meant. Robyn could hardly believe he would go to such lengths.

'Robyn.' His voice softened to a more persuasive tone. 'I know you're not close to your own family. I know you don't want me around you. But I don't want you worried by personal concerns. If you're sick or distressed, you'll have Tina on hand to help you, and if you find that you don't like Tina, just call me and I'll find someone else.'

Robyn's inner tension eased a little. She could see now that Julian was trying to solve problems that could very well lie ahead of her, and ease her loneliness in the most inoffensive way. He wasn't to know that she had worked things out with her mother. And at least he did not intend to push himself into her life. She was grateful for his forbearance on that score, even though he misunderstood her motives for wanting to avoid his company.

'And you'll be satisfied that I'm looking after myself if I accept Tina. Is that the case, Julian?' she asked cautiously, not at all sure that he didn't have something else up his sleeve.

His half-smile was more in the nature of a grimace. 'Not satisfied, no. But trying for the impossible is hardly likely to earn your co-operation. It's not my intention to alienate you any further, Robyn. Tina is the bottom line. But I do hope that you and I can come to a better understanding some time before the child is born.'

She nodded wearily, thinking how very clever he was to have worked the situation out along the lines she had drawn herself. But of course Julian had always known what to say to her to achieve the desired result. A few wrong words from him and she might not have married David. But that was water under the bridge, and Julian was right, there was no turning back now.

'Well, if you've brought this Tina Stavlikos with you, bring her in. I'll give her a try,' she conceded carelessly.

'One more thing, Robyn.' He hesitated, for the first time seemingly unsure of himself. His face was twisted with the ravaging of inner torment. 'You must understand... I've got to make sure myself that everything is all right with you. I'll be coming to see you from time to time.'

'No!' Robyn punched the word out with all the vehemence of her own torment.

'Not so often as to distress you,' Julian argued, his eyes stabbing his need at her. 'I wouldn't do anything that might harm the baby.'

'No!' Her protest was all the more passionate at his mention of the baby. She could hardly bear his love for David's child when she wanted his love so desperately for herself.

She glared at him, hiding the hurt behind mutinous determination. 'I'm not a fool, Julian. I'm quite capable of looking after myself. However, I'll accept your nursemaid to ensure your peace of mind. But that's all. I won't have you dropping in on me whenever you feel like it. Or whenever it's convenient to you.'

He went white. 'I can't permit you to cut me out of the child's life like that, Robyn.'

Tears rushed into her eyes and she covered them with her hand as she struggled once more for control. 'I don't intend to do that, Julian,' she forced out in weary resignation. 'But there's no need for you to... to check on me personally while I'm pregnant. I'll call you if there's anything wrong. If anything goes wrong.' She raised bleak, tear-washed eyes. 'You'll just have to trust me to do that.'

'Robyn.' He stretched out his hands in tortured appeal, and for a moment the agony of that last night on Maui was a living, writhing thing between them. 'Is there nothing more I can do for you?'

She shook her head, unable to speak, anguished by the tumult of feeling that cried out for him to have been the man who had made love to her. Her gaze dropped to his mouth, his throat, the strong breadth of his chest, and fastened blindly on the striped tie that hid his shirt-buttons. She saw his chest rise and fall in a quick, shallow breath.

'So be it!' he muttered, but his tight tone held more a note of challenge than resignation. And steely purpose lent another edge to his voice as he added, 'I'll go and get Tina. She's waiting in my car.'

Robyn shut her eyes and nodded, needing some respite from Julian's presence in order to pull herself out of the madness that possessed her. It was David's child she was carrying. And some time in the next eight months she had to learn to think of Julian as a brother.

She rubbed a hand across her forehead, wishing she could wipe out the feverish thoughts that persisted against all common sense. Pride insisted that she meet this woman Julian was bringing to her with some semblance of self-command. She pushed herself out of the armchair, forced her shaky legs to walk into the office, then resettled herself on the chair behind her desk, hoping she could achieve a businesslike manner.

She heard them at the door and called out to draw them into the office. It was a relief to hear that her voice sounded reasonably calm, but her heart gave a nasty lurch when Julian ushered the woman into the room.

Tina Stavlikos was stunningly attractive. Her face held the best of classic Greek features, cast in the smoothest of olive skins. Glossy black hair rippled luxuriantly to her shoulders, and her black business suit did nothing to detract from her tall, statuesque figure. Her huge, liquid brown eyes surveyed Robyn with cautious reserve, but the wide, sensual mouth curved into a winning smile as Julian performed the introductions.

'I'm very happy to meet you, Mrs Lassiter.'

'Please, call me Robyn.' She might be David's wife but she didn't want to be reminded of the fact every minute of the day. She managed a stiff smile. 'I hope you don't mind if I call you Tina.'

'Not at all.' Her mouth widened into an infectious grin. 'Stavlikos is a mouthful.'

Robyn nodded, too conscious of Julian watching her to give any natural responses. She met his gaze with tightly guarded control. 'You can leave Tina here now, Julian.'

The hazel-green eyes held an intense need that burned down into her soul. 'You will call me, Robyn, for anything at all.'

'I said I would, Julian,' Robyn answered tersely, reacting to the tension that throbbed between them.

He didn't want to accept it. Didn't want to go. For several nerve-tearing moments Robyn thought he wouldn't. Then he slowly exhaled a long breath and stabbed a glance at Tina. He didn't say a word. There was no need to. Robyn sensed their mutual understanding. And resented it.

'Then I'll say goodbye... for now,' he directed back at Robyn, his eyes hooding whatever feelings he had on the situation.

'Thank you for your thoughtfulness,' Robyn said with formal politeness.

'Anything at all, Robyn,' he reminded her huskily, and took his leave without more ado.

She listened for the front door to close, every fibre of her being straining to run after him, to beg for things that were impossible. The door clicked shut and the pain in her heart was so intense that it was several moments before she could force her attention on to the woman Julian had left behind.

'Sit down, Tina,' she said flatly.

The woman took the chair closest to Robyn's desk. There were anxious little lines about her huge, watchful eyes, and she wasn't as young as Robyn had first thought; possibly in her late thirties. But Julian was also in his late thirties, and Tina was obviously in his confidence.

Robyn couldn't stop the claws of jealousy from digging into her heart. Was Tina Stavlikos one of Julian's 'casual relationships'? She had to know. 'Julian said you come from his personal staff. Are you a special friend of his?' she asked.

'Of course not!' Tina was obviously surprised by the question. 'We respect each other's abilities. But neither Mr Lassiter nor I have ever thought of maintaining a friendship outside work.'

'You're very attractive, Tina,' Robyn observed, unable to shake herself free from the thought that this woman had enjoyed a closer and longer association with Julian than she herself had ever had.

Tina smiled. 'I doubt whether Mr Lassiter has ever noticed. Apart from his wife, I've never seen him show any awareness of a woman, until...' She stopped and looked somewhat ill at ease. 'I think you mean a great deal to him, but that is none of my business.'

Aware of her! The words recalled the first time they had laid eyes on each other. The attraction had been there from the start. She had struggled against it. Julian had rejected it. And that dangerous moment in the stretch limousine... But David's happiness had been more important to him. And she—in her ignorance—had agreed. Too late now.

But Tina's comment did give her an opening to probe that part of Julian's life which she most wanted to know about. 'I never met Julian's wife,' she said, trying to project idle curiosity. 'What was she like?'

Tina frowned, picking her words carefully. 'I couldn't say I knew Vanessa Lassiter. I saw her a few times at the office, and at company dinners. She was, without a doubt, the most beautiful woman I've ever seen in the flesh. You had to keep looking at her. Everyone did. But...' Tina hesitated, shrugging as she gave Robyn a woman-to-woman smile, 'I didn't like her.'

'Too beautiful?' Robyn prompted.

'Too knowing,' Tina corrected. 'She knew the power her beauty gave her and loved it. She lapped up the reactions she drew from people and always played for more.'

'So that's why she didn't want to spoil her figure by having children,' Robyn murmured.

'And why she committed suicide.'

Robyn looked at Tina in absolute shock. 'Suicide?'

Tina's face flushed at the realisation of her indiscretion. 'I thought you knew.'

Robyn shook her head. 'Only that she had died. Why on earth would she have committed suicide?'

Tina's grimace was one of distaste, but she knew she had gone too far not to answer now. 'They said it was depression after the accident. She was at a party and a gas-barbecue blew up. Her face and shoulders were scarred by fire, and apparently plastic surgery couldn't restore the flawless beauty that had been hers. She took an overdose of drugs.'

'How dreadful!' Robyn whispered. Yet she could not help thinking that it explained so much about Julian: his bitterness and his cynicism about women, his softening towards her when she had agreed to have David's child.

She remembered him saying on that last night before he and David left Maui that she had changed his feelings about women for ever. And his distraught manner as he spoke of his miscalculation in marrying her to David, how much he regretted everything.

A wild hope stirred in Robyn's heart. If he was aware of her in the same way as he had been aware of his wife... Robyn's thoughts whirled into tormenting chaos again.

For several moments she even forgot that Tina Stavlikos was in the room. The other woman pulled her back to present realities with a tactful change of subject.

'I'd love to hear more about your business, Robyn. From what Mr Lassiter said, it sounds as if it has lots of scope for development.' Her mouth widened into the infectious grin again. 'And I do so enjoy challenges.'

Robyn pulled herself together and forced herself to review the situation. Although she had told Julian that she didn't need help in her business, perhaps it would be pleasant to have Tina at her side, to talk over her ideas, share her work, and possibly learn a lot about Julian that she wouldn't know otherwise.

Apart from that, she hadn't been able to concentrate on any work at all lately. And, if she didn't settle into something positive soon, she might easily go mad thinking of other things.

On a wave of firm decisiveness, Robyn suggested that Tina bring her chair around so that they could share the desk. And, for the first time since the Lassiters had invaded her life, Robyn spent several hours without a thought for either one of them.

It was only when Tina left for the day that Robyn's mind turned once more to Julian, and depression rolled over her. There was no point in wondering what he felt for her. As he had said this morning, it had gone too far and there was no turning back now. David's child stood between them.

And those two fateful nights! How could she forget them? Yet still she couldn't connect them to David. And she couldn't bear to face either man. It hurt too much. She was having the baby. That was all she could manage as far as the Lassiter family was concerned.

As one week dragged into another, Robyn found that, however dark some of her nights were, getting through the days was relatively easy with Tina. Not only was Tina's business acumen impressive—she found new outlets for Robyn's tourist packages and sold them with amazing success—but also her natural enthusiasm for everything made her an invigorating companion.

Robyn's life moved into a new phase—one of revitalised interest in her work, and a new closeness with her mother and sisters.

Weeks worked their way into months. Robyn didn't know what her mother had told her sisters, but they came calling on her. Barbara and her husband brought over a cot and toys. Jodie brought a pile of nappies and baby clothes, and urged Robyn to pick out some patterns for matinée jackets because she loved knitting baby things and would really enjoy doing them for her.

Both her sisters seemed genuinely glad to see her and to be of help. They got so much pleasure out of supplying these articles that Robyn couldn't refuse them. With the Lassiter wealth behind her, she could have bought anything at all for her child, but the spirit behind her sisters' gifts completely overwhelmed her and the re-tying of family bonds was too important to gainsay.

Neither Barbara nor Jodie criticised her. In fact they regarded what she had done almost with awe. But they were on firm and familiar ground with pregnancies and babies, and were happy that Robyn was at last sharing this experience with them. They made a frequent habit of calling to check up on her and offer advice, and their caring was a growing pleasure for Robyn.

Certainly the consequences of having David's baby were far from being all negative. If Julian had not existed, Robyn would have been happier than she had ever been in her life. But Julian did exist, and so did the yearning ache for him that nothing could appease.

Thousands of times she was tempted to call him and fought to put the temptation aside. She had no reason to contact him at all. And she didn't, until after her doctor had sent her for an ultra-sound scan. Even then she vacillated for several days. There was nothing wrong with her or the baby. She didn't have to give the photograph to David, but she thought it might mean a lot to him and it was the right thing to do in the circumstances.

Of course, she could post it to Julian with instructions to pass it on to David. She didn't have to hand it to Julian personally. But it was something precious, too precious to risk to the post, she argued. And one short visit couldn't hurt her too much. If she could control her feelings, she might even be able to judge how much she meant to Julian.

But somehow, she couldn't take the irrevocable step of actually calling him. She didn't want to hear his disembodied voice on the telephone. In the end, she used Tina, pretending it meant nothing to her at all.

'By the way,' she said casually one afternoon as Tina was getting ready to leave, 'when you next speak to Julian, tell him I'd like to see him.'

Tina sliced her an oddly wary look and Robyn reacted with resentful aggressiveness before she could catch back the words. 'Let's not pretend, Tina. Your job is to report to him, isn't it? However much you do for me.'

'I like the work I do with you, Robyn. But yes, Mr Lassiter does ring me every night to ask after you.'

'Every night?' Robyn repeated incredulously.

Tina nodded, obviously apprehensive about giving away anything that Robyn might find offensive.

Robyn shook her head in surprise. She hadn't realised that Julian would be quite so diligent about her welfare.

'He worries about you,' Tina offered cautiously. 'I try to reassure him. That's all it is, Robyn.'

'What are you, Tina? I mean, really,' Robyn asked, amazed at the depth of trust Julian placed in her. 'What position did you hold on Julian's staff before he hijacked you to look after me?'

Her shrug tried to minimise her importance. 'I was his chief trouble-shooter. The Lassiter Corporation has various business interests around the world. I went wherever there was a problem, sorted it out, then came home and reported on it.'

Robyn's smile was all irony. 'So I'm Julian's problem now. My business must have been small potatoes to you, Tina. What a waste of your talent!'

Tina hesitated, frowned, then looked Robyn straight in the eye. 'Don't underestimate yourself, Robyn. I don't have your gift for conceptual thinking. And without your gift, I'd have nothing to sell. I'm a good entrepreneur, that's all. And I've enjoyed this job more than any I've had.' Her generous mouth widened into its infectious grin. 'No problems!'

Robyn had to laugh and Tina joined in, their easy, relaxed relationship quickly restored.

But Robyn could not stay relaxed after Tina departed for the day. If what Tina had told her about Julian's obsession with her welfare was true, and Robyn had no reason to doubt it, then the probability was he would call on her this evening.

It was madness to indulge in making herself attractive for him, but Robyn couldn't help herself. She showered and washed her hair, then spent a long time with the blow-dryer, styling her thick blonde hair into a bouncy frame for her face. She applied only a little unobtrusive make-up. Her skin was blooming with health, anyway— one of the best side-effects of pregnancy, Jodie had assured her.

But her figure had certainly suffered; her waist thickened with each month that passed—almost four months now. She had bought slacks with elasticised waists and she selected the grey-blue pair which she teamed with a loose overblouse patterned with tiny pink and blue flowers. It was a particularly feminine outfit and Robyn was satisfied that she looked as good as she could.

It was just past eight o'clock when the doorbell rang, and Robyn didn't have to check through the peephole to know it was Julian. Her pulse instantly lost all regularity. Her cheeks burnt with a hot rush of blood. Her legs turned to water. And she knew she had been an absolute fool to imagine she could repress her feelings for him. But it was too late to change her mind now. She took a deep breath and opened the door.

The hopeful anticipation in his eyes twisted her heart and his choice of clothes was an obvious attempt to put this meeting on an informal, more friendly basis. Unfortunately, they brought even more attention to his attraction.

The dark red shirt lent another dimension to the distinctive cut of his face and threw the thick blackness of his hair into devastating contrast; and the close-fitting fawn trousers stirred a fluttering awareness of his powerful physique.

'Tina said you wanted to see me,' he prompted when Robyn failed to greet him.

She forced her tongue to work. 'Yes. Yes, I did. Come in, Julian.'

He followed her into the sitting-room and when she invited him to sit down, hoping to diminish his dominating impact on her, he did as she asked. But there was no abatement of the tension emanating from him as he settled on the two-seater sofa. His eyes ran over her with a hungry intensity, as if he could not bear to let any detail of her appearance escape him.

'You look well, Robyn,' he said with strained softness.

'I am. Well, I mean.' She perched on the edge of an armchair, too tense herself to relax. 'Tina's been doing a good job of looking after me. I like her very much. I'm grateful to you for giving her to me.'

'It was the least I could do,' he murmured. 'Is there anything...?'

'No,' she said quickly. 'I don't want to ask for anything. I want to give you something.'

His eyebrows lifted in puzzled enquiry.

Embarrassment sent another hot spurt of colour into Robyn's cheeks. 'It's not for you, exactly. It's for David. Is he...all right?'

Julian instantly hooded his eyes and his eyebrows lowered into a dark frown. 'You know Davey doesn't expect anything from you, Robyn. Other than what you're doing. He's coping quite well...in the circumstances.'

It was a stiff little speech, scraping over a lot of raw memories, and Robyn wished she hadn't asked the question.

'He'll want this, I think. I'll just go and get it from the office.'

To Robyn's consternation Julian rose and followed her into the adjoining room. She had left the manila envelope on the desk ready, and she quickly snatched it up and passed it to him, afraid to let him get too close to her. Her heart was thumping madly as it was.

'My doctor sent me for an ultra-sound scan last week,' she explained, looking down at what she was giving away. However reluctant she was to part with it, she still felt it was the right thing to do. She didn't need it. In another few months she would have the reality.

'It's a photograph...of the baby. Not very decipherable, but David is a scientist, and he'd know, and understand.'

One of Julian's hands slid to the flap, fingering it as if he wanted to open it, but then gripped tightly and was still. 'It's very generous of you, Robyn,' he said huskily.

'There's something else he may want to know,' Robyn added hesitantly. 'I'm not sure he'll be so pleased, but...' she lifted her eyes, wanting to see how Julian reacted '...the baby is a girl.'

The tense strain on his face gave way to a slow glow of radiant pleasure. 'A daughter...'

Robyn felt a wild and unreasonable rush of relief that Julian had not shown disappointment. It had not mattered to her what sex the baby was—if it was born healthy, what did it matter?—but it had nagged at her mind that David and Julian might have set their hearts on a male child.

Not Julian, certainly. He obviously didn't care. He looked like the proudest father on earth. Except he wasn't the father, Robyn reminded herself, and tried to smother the pain that accompanied the inescapable truth. It was David's child—the only child he would ever have—and Robyn wanted him to feel as delighted as she did about a daughter.

'Julian, when you tell David, remind him that Madame Curie and her daughter both won Nobel Prizes in chemistry. Females can do it. And his daughter can too, if she has David's ability.'

Julian laughed and shook his head. 'It doesn't matter. Not a damn. Even if she never looks at a science-book, how could it matter? A child! What a miracle!' His eyes seemed to be looking far off at some unknown promised land. His smile was one of pure, undiluted happiness. His voice caressed the word again. 'A daughter...'

The way he said it...Robyn's mind and heart were savaged again by doubts. She had been so certain it was Julian who had made love to her, and his reaction now was surely that of a father, not an uncle. It had been him, she thought wildly. It had to have been him making love to her on those two fateful nights! And that was why he was aware of her, and so obsessed with her welfare! It was his child, not David's!

And the pain rolled back again, more devastating than ever with the realisation that he intended the deception to go on. In that moment she hated him with a blistering hatred. How could he have denied it? How could he keep denying it?

She turned her back on him, seething with angry bitterness. 'That's all I wanted you for, Julian,' she said through gritted teeth, wanting him to pay for what he had done, to feel the same depth of rejection she had. He was betraying her and his child, for his brother's sake!

And yet... David had to know that the baby wasn't his. Why had he told his mother that Robyn might be having his child, a child that would inherit his estate? What was behind it all? None of it made any sense to her!

'Robyn...'

The soft call throbbed with deeply felt emotion. Her heart lurched as his hand fell gently on her shoulder, drawing her around to face him. Sheer chaos broke out inside her when the hand lifted to stroke her cheek. His touch...Julian...Julian, her heart whispered as she stared fixedly at the open-necked V of his shirt. The pulse in his throat seemed to beat as erratically as her own.

Was he going to tell her the truth? Admit to the deception and confess what had really happened?

'I just wanted to say...'

Robyn held her breath, waiting, hoping, willing him to tell her that he couldn't go on, that he loved her.

His voice was a soft caress. 'As far as I'm concerned, not all the Nobel Prizes in the world could honour you enough for the person you are, for your humanity, and courage, and generosity. You are unique, Robyn. No one else could measure up to you.'

The steel band around her chest collapsed as her pent-up breath rushed out on a wave of terrible disillusionment. Julian's words were all too pointed in telling her that any feelings he had for her were related to what she had done for his brother.

She tore herself out of his gentle hold and marched blindly to the front door. 'Thank you for coming,' she recited stiffly when Julian finally followed her.

'Robyn . . .'

'Tell David I wish him well,' she threw at him, desperate for Julian to go without any argument, before she threw the most horrific accusations at him. Accusations for which she had no proof except her own turbulent feelings.

He paused by her for several nerveracking moments but Robyn refused to look up at him. Maybe she was mad. It must have been David, and it had to be David's baby, but she couldn't bear to look at Julian again anyway.

He sighed heavily and stepped past her. 'Goodnight, Robyn. Sleep well,' he said in soft benediction.

She couldn't answer. All she could do was close the door and keep it closed on Julian Lassiter. She simply couldn't cope with the pain he stirred.

CHAPTER THIRTEEN

THE months that followed were difficult for Robyn. The discomfort of morning sickness gave way to other more stressful discomforts: a persistent backache that came with the changing balance of her hitherto slim body, a fatigue that sapped her will to do anything that required much energy, and an uncharacteristic clumsiness of movement that had her stubbing her toes and dropping things.

But there was the surprising joy of feeling the baby move inside her; and that countered the pain of thinking about Julian and David. She did not call Julian again, and he placed no pressure on her to let him come.

She did less and less work as her pregnancy progressed. Tina insisted that all Robyn had to do was the creative thinking, and she was happy to do the rest. More than happy. Positively eager. She enjoyed the work, she said, and insisted that Robyn had widened her horizons with all she had learnt from her about other countries and cultures.

Robyn was increasingly conscious of time passing: five months, six months as Christmas approached, and there was no word from Julian about David. Robyn didn't know what to think. If David was the father of her baby, and surely her feelings for Julian had misled her into imagining otherwise, then she couldn't simply ignore him.

She agonised over whether she should ask Julian to take her to visit his brother, but that had not been in the agreement and she shied away from the painful complications of another meeting. But the more she thought about David and his illness, the more agitated she became about not knowing what was happening with him. In the end she used Tina in exactly the same way as Julian used her.

'Next time you report to Julian, ask him for a report on David. Tell him I want to know how he is.'

'Why don't you call him yourself, Robyn?' Tina suggested quietly. 'I'm sure Mr Lassiter would like you to.'

'No!' Robyn retorted sharply, then sighed as she saw the concerned look on Tina's face. 'It's better this way, believe me, Tina. Please, be my go-between, as well as Julian's.'

Tactful as always, Tina asked no more questions. She reported back that David was fighting on, using all his will-power to live until his daughter was born. He was determined not to die without first seeing his child.

Tears rushed into Robyn's eyes. She had been wrong. The baby she was carrying had to be David's or he wouldn't be clinging so tenaciously to life to see a child that was not his. And again the compassion that had drawn her into accepting David's proposition in the first place flooded through her.

What David was going through made her own problems seem petty, and she hoped that he would live long enough to hold their daughter in his arms.

She was sorely tempted to call Julian. Often her hand was only inches from the telephone before her resolution would come back. It could only be painful to her. To Julian, she was only a means to an end, bringing a child into the world for David. All his caring concern and admiration for her were founded on what she was doing for David. She had fantasised too much that was wrong to try getting closer to him. Better for her to consolidate her own life.

Christmas came, and for the first time in too many years to remember, Robyn spent a very happy day with her family. Henry Brownlow, her mother's indulgent bridge-partner from the senior citizens' club, shared it with them and very proudly announced that Marjorie had consented to marry him. In a rather nervous aside, her mother asked Robyn if she liked him, obviously anxious for her approval, and Robyn had no hesitation at all in replying that whatever made her mother happy was fine by her.

January slipped into February. Robyn practised what she was taught at the pre-natal clinic. The last few weeks of her pregnancy caused Robyn an immense amount of distress. David was still alive, clinging to his life beyond all the doctors' expectations. He had been transferred to the hospital where Robyn was to have the baby, and it caused Robyn much anguish to think that the baby might not come in time. She even wondered if she should ask her doctor to induce the birth rather than let it go overdue.

However, before she had made any positive step towards discussing the matter with Julian, the baby decided the question for her. The first pain of labour awakened Robyn near dawn one morning, ten days before the birth was due. She dismissed it as just another advanced-pregnancy discomfort. But the next pain an hour later made her wonder, and the next sent a fierce hope through her that this was not a false alarm and the baby really was making a purposeful move.

By the time Tina arrived for work, Robyn was almost certain that it was finally happening. She had had five contractions, fairly regularly spaced, and as soon as she told her friend about them, Tina brushed away any doubt and grabbed the telephone.

With the brilliant efficiency that Tina brought to everything, she quickly alerted the doctor, the hospital, and Julian. Then she checked that Robyn had everything she needed before calmly driving her to the hospital.

Julian met them there, his face pale and drawn. He asked Tina to do the official checking in and took Robyn's arm to help her into the reception area.

'How's David?' she asked.

'Waiting,' he answered grimly.

Another contraction hit her and she automatically hunched over, wincing from the pain. Julian's arm came around her instantly in support.

'I'm all right,' she gasped, trembling in reaction as he hugged her close to him. She glanced up, agonised that he should still have such a devastating effect on her after all this time.

His arm tightened about her and ruthless determination looked back at her. 'I'm going through this with you, Robyn. You're not going to be alone.'

'You don't have to worry about me, Julian. I've been alone before. And this will be over soon enough. I'll cope. I have with everything else.' Miserable resignation dulled her voice as she dragged her gaze away from him. 'And then you and David will both have what you want.'

'Davey might ... but I won't. Without you, I'll never have what I want.'

The impassioned words throbbed through Robyn's heart, forcing her to look up at him again. His face was strained, his eyes darkly haunted with needs that stripped her defences.

'What more do you want of me?' she cried in pained protest.

'I want you to marry me!'

'No ... no ...' she groaned as her need for him conflicted with the knowledge that what he really wanted was the child. 'You can't mean that!'

'But I do!' he insisted vehemently.

She shook her head in helpless defeat. 'You don't have to sacrifice yourself, Julian. I won't keep you away any more. You can see David's child as often as you like. Do what you like. Marriage doesn't have to come into it.'

'It does for me! All these months of being cut out of your life have been hell, a wasteland, a void, pointless and without meaning. I can't bear it any more. If I can't have you, I might as well be dead.'

'Don't say that!' she cried, her hand racing up to cover the strong beat of his heart. She didn't know what to think. He spoke with such terrible passion, but ... 'It's only because of the baby ... because of David.'

'No!' His hand covered hers, crushing it to him. 'I love you, Robyn. Without you, every day is a torment, an emptiness.'

'You hardly know me.'

'I know all about you, what makes you smile and laugh, what makes you sad, what you've done and said. I've lived to hear about you every night, and then be tortured because you wouldn't let me near you to comfort you when you were unhappy, to be at your side helping in any way I could. I know you, Robyn, and if you'll only let me love you, I swear I'll make you happy.'

She couldn't take it in. All these months of wanting him, loving him, and he felt the same? But how could he? How could he have married her to David? Or had Julian come to love her afterwards?

Another contraction sawed through her body and she doubled up. Julian caught her and eased her on to a chair.

'Robyn.' His anguish reached into her and tore around her heart, forcing her to re-evaluate. 'At least let me stay with you while the baby is born.'

'Will the hospital let you?' She needed to understand Julian, to know what motives drove him to this bewildering proposal.

The muscles along his jaw tightened. 'If you say yes, it doesn't matter a damn what anyone else says. Wild horses couldn't drag me away from your side.' And the look of reckless determination on his face underlined his need to be with her.

'Then you can stay.'

Robyn didn't have time to consider his relief at this concession from her. Tina came back to them, the hospital's paperwork completed, bringing with her a nurse with a wheelchair. Julian and the nurse helped Robyn into it, and Tina took her leave, promising to telephone Robyn's mother and reassure her that everything was taken care of.

The nurse wheeled Robyn to a preparation room and insisted that Julian wait outside until Robyn was ready to be taken to the labour ward. It gave Robyn some time to think by herself and she badly needed it.

Did Julian truly love her as he claimed, or had he become obsessed with her because she was having David's child? She desperately wanted to believe him, but if she married him and found out afterwards it was another disastrous mistake, how on earth would she cope with living through such a travesty of the marriage she really wanted?

How could she gauge what he truly felt? He had never even kissed her, except on her forehead. Tina had said he was aware of her as a woman, as he had been with his wife, but that had been after he knew she was carrying a child. She tried to remember the times before, but all their meetings had been concentrated on issues that overshadowed everything else.

Robyn was still in a state of painful confusion when the nurse finished with her and helped her on to a bed which was to be wheeled to the labour ward. Julian was waiting in the corridor outside, and the sight of him and his concern for her almost made Robyn throw caution to the winds and accept his proposal on the spot. But there were too many questions unanswered.

The nurse saw Robyn comfortably settled in the ward, showed her the button to press for attention, then left her alone with Julian. He pulled a chair up beside her bed and picked up one of her hands, pressing it in agitated feeling.

'Is there anything I can do, Robyn?' he asked anxiously.

'Yes.' But a wave of pain made her gasp and it was several seconds before she had the breath to speak again. He watched her in white-faced anguish and she squeezed his hand in reassurance. 'I can't think right now...of marrying you, Julian. I...'

'No. Of course not,' he cut in brusquely. 'I'm sorry for troubling you when...' He swallowed hard. 'Just you concentrate on having the baby, Robyn. Everything else can wait.'

It should have been his baby, Robyn thought with a twist of the old pain. Even now, when she knew better, it was hard to accept that David was the one. It had been Julian in her mind, always Julian.

'Do you really want this baby, Robyn?' he asked huskily.

'Yes. Very much,' she answered with conviction. It was her baby, even if it wasn't his.

Julian looked relieved. 'It's worried me so much, that you could never forgive me, my part in making this happen.'

She gripped his hand tight as another contraction started and she waited until she had breathed her way through it.

'It wasn't all your doing, Julian. I was willing.'

He shook his head, unconsoled. 'You were so hurt. And now this. And I can't relieve your distress any more now than I could then,' he cried in pained frustration.

'It helps to have you with me,' she soothed. 'Somehow it feels right. We started this together, didn't we? A child for David.'

'Robyn.' His eyes searched hers with urgent intensity. 'You don't mind any more?'

'No.' She smiled to reassure him, but the smile turned into a wince as another wave of pain hit her.

'I'll make it up to you. I swear I'll make all this up to you, Robyn,' Julian declared passionately.

Robyn's fingers dug reflexively into his hand. 'Don't feel guilty. I don't want you to feel guilty,' she begged. If that was why he had asked her to marry him, how could she possibly be happy, knowing he was only trying to compensate for what she had gone through for his brother?

'Tell me what you do want.' It was a cry from the heart, desperate to please.

'I want you to share this with me. Not looking back, Julian, but forward. There should be joy in this birth. For you and me...and David. It's what we've all been waiting for. No more pain, Julian.'

He drew in a deep breath and tried to relax. 'A beautiful little girl,' he said fervently.

'Yes,' she agreed.

And the beautiful little girl made another move towards birth, testing any sense of joy to the limit.

But Julian did not waver from supporting her throughout the hard hours of labour that followed. He encouraged her, calmed her with soothing words, tenderly stroked her hair away from her clammy forehead and held her hand, lending her his strength when she clung more and more desperately to him as each pain sliced into the last.

And Robyn knew that if he could have taken her agony upon himself, he would have, so intense was his empathy with every wave of pain that brought the birth closer and closer. They were together, sharing an experience that was even more intimate than lovemaking, and Robyn wished again that the baby were his.

But they would have other babies...if she married him. And of course she would. How could she not? She loved him far too much to refuse him anything. And she would give him the children that his other wife had denied him.

The pain suddenly changed to a deep dragging at her lower body, and the nurse who had been in attendance for some time summoned the matron. Robyn's doctor came in and started giving her instructions. She responded automatically to what he told her, but only Julian really existed for her.

And she went beyond hiding what she felt for him. The love in her heart spilled into her eyes, reached out to him, and seemed to be returned with anguished feeling. Neither of them spoke a word, but their hands clung more tightly as the long-awaited child came into the world, and they smiled as they heard its first cry.

'She's here,' Robyn whispered.

'Yes,' Julian breathed.

'Bring her to me.'

He drew in a shaky breath and stood up, reluctantly releasing her hand.

The umbilical cord had to be cut, the baby washed and tagged and wrapped in a comforting bunny-rug. But when the nurse finally placed the precious bundle in Julian's arms, Robyn knew she would cherish for ever the look of wondrous pleasure that softened his face as he looked down at her new-born baby. And in that moment was born the certainty that he would love her daughter as though she were his own, always and for ever.

'She's got red hair,' he said, as if that was a remarkable achievement instead of a matter of direct inheritance from David.

And David was waiting.

A look of poignant understanding passed between them. This moment belonged to them in one sense, they had done what they had set out to do, but now it had to be completed.

'Let me see her,' Robyn said softly.

Julian placed the baby in her arms. Robyn smiled down at the crumpled little face and ran a soft finger over the red-gold down that covered the tiny head.

'She is beautiful, isn't she?' she breathed adoringly.

'Incredibly beautiful,' Julian agreed with no less feeling.

Robyn hugged her close, savouring the wonderful rush of maternal love that swamped the strange emptiness after the birth. It was hard to give up her baby now that she held her, but Robyn knew she had all the tomorrows to spend on loving the child who nestled so naturally in her arms.

'Take her to David now, Julian,' she said firmly. 'We can't keep him waiting any longer.'

And he read the compassion that demanded he do her bidding and he took the child to his brother.

The labour of birth had been long and exhausting, and Robyn slept with the peace of fulfilment in her heart. She had done what David had wanted. She had her daughter. And perhaps Julian really did love her. Certainly he loved her child.

It was dark when she awoke. She felt a weight pressing against her side and it took several moments for her eyes to make out the hunch of shoulders over the bed. She knew instinctively that it was Julian, his arms resting on the bedcover, his head slumped over them. And she knew he wasn't asleep.

She didn't stop to question the thought. It came to her with a certainty that couldn't be questioned, and she curled her hand over the grieving head in silent sympathy as she spoke. 'He's gone, hasn't he?'

'Yes,' Julian choked.

'Were we in time?'

'Yes.'

And he wept. He wept with the tortured agony of a strong man who didn't want to weep but couldn't help himself. And Robyn dragged him into her arms and held him to her heart, her soothing hands telling him what words could not: that his pain was hers, and she loved him all the more for sharing it with her.

It was a long time before his laboured gasps eased to a more controlled breathing, but even then he didn't move away from her. Robyn cradled his head against the soft fullness of her breasts and kept stroking his hair.

'Davey loved the baby, Robyn. The look in his eyes . . . the smile when he cradled her in his arms . . . he said it was worth it all . . . every last minute of pain.'

'Then it was worth it, wasn't it?' she said softly, feeling a strange and beautiful peace as she thought of David holding their daughter, passing on the breath of his life. *Aloha*, my child!

'I hope so,' Julian sighed, and dragged himself out of her compassionate embrace. He picked up her hand and fondled it gently. 'I hope it was right for him. I hope I can make it right for you.'

He lifted her hand, pressed a soft, yearning kiss on to her palm, then held it against his cheek. 'I need you, Robyn.' The hoarse whisper was dragged from a heart that had carried too heavy a burden all these months, and Robyn's response was just as direct and heartfelt.

'I need you, too.'

And she did. Even if she couldn't have him as she wanted him, she needed him in her life, to hold her hand over the rough patches, however bitter-sweet that might be. He was a good man. A loving man. And she would take whatever he wanted to give her.

'I will marry you, Julian,' she said firmly.

His head jerked up, and when he let her hand drop in his surprise, he quickly grasped it with both of his, holding it like a prayer of entreaty. 'Robyn, I swear to you I'll make you a good husband, and a father to your child. I'll love the baby as if she were my own.'

She didn't have to be told that. 'And me?' she asked. 'Will you love me, Julian?'

'All my life!' he replied with fervent conviction. 'And I will make it right for you, Robyn. I'll make it right if it's the last thing I do.'

It sounded like a vow, and she wondered if it was, if David had asked this of him. And she remembered David's words on their wedding day: 'I give you into my brother's keeping.'

Other words came echoing out of her memory—Julian warning her on the night he outlined the proposition—'It won't be over in a few moments, or a few days, or even with Davey's death. You will be living with the consequences for the rest of your life.'

She sighed and stroked his hand. 'It's been . . . quite a night. Birth, death, marriage. Somehow it seems inevitable.'

'Robyn.' He squeezed her hand hard. 'You won't change your mind tomorrow?'

'No. I won't change my mind. For better or for worse, Julian.'

And it was inevitable. She knew that now.

A smile curved her mouth as she remembered that this was the marriage the old lady had predicted.

The greatest sadness, and then the greatest happiness.

So surely it would be all right in time.

It had to be so.

CHAPTER FOURTEEN

ROBYN decided to call her daughter Faith. The name seemed just right for the child who embodied so many hopes for the future. And Julian agreed with the choice, saying it was exactly what David would have wanted. Robyn asked him to pick a second name, and after some consideration he suggested Dominique, saying that if ever there was a child of the Lord, it was this one.

Faith Dominique Lassiter... Robyn liked it, and so it was decided.

Robyn's mother and sisters came with gifts and clucked over the new baby as if she were their own. They were astonished by Faith's red hair and Robyn had to explain that she had inherited her father's colouring. It shocked them to hear that David had died on the same night that Faith had been born, but since they had never met him the shock was mitigated by Robyn's contentment that he had seen his daughter.

She did not tell them about the proposed marriage between herself and Julian. There would be a more appropriate time for that later. Julian wanted to marry as soon as they could arrange it, but they had both reluctantly agreed on a three-month waiting period. Under the circumstances, that was the shortest possible period consistent with considering the sensibilities of both families.

Apart from which, this time Robyn wanted to be absolutely sure what her marriage to Julian would entail before she revealed her own deep feelings towards him. She had gone blindly ahead once. She didn't intend to do it twice. This time she would be more prepared for whatever lay ahead of her.

Although it had been long anticipated, David's death had hit his parents hard, and it was left to Julian to shoulder the responsibility of settling his brother's affairs. He snatched what time he could to visit Robyn, and, since she was in a private room at the hospital, there were no restrictions on when he had to arrive or leave.

But she knew that the shock of David's death had hit Julian hard, too. Robyn realised that the knowledge that an event was going to happen didn't minimise the impact when it did occur. She made no demands on him, and Julian seemed satisfied merely to be with her and the baby.

Mostly he kissed Robyn on the forehead or cheek in greeting, sometimes the merest brush of his lips across hers, but he looked at her with love. Robyn worried whether it was the same kind of love he gave to her daughter, or was he merely practising restraint until a more appropriate time? If he felt desire for her, he certainly didn't show it.

The funeral took place while Robyn was still in hospital. She had a sheaf of 'Peace' roses sent, with a card that read simply, 'Thank you.'

The next day brought a surprise meeting. Robyn had just finished breast-feeding Faith, and the baby was cradled contentedly in her arms when a tentative knock drew her attention. Janet Lassiter stood in the doorway with a tall, white-haired man who had enough of Julian about him for Robyn to recognise him as Wade Lassiter,

Julian's father. Both of them were stiff with tension, and Janet's distress was patent as she looked despairingly at Robyn and the baby.

'May we come in?' Wade asked, clearly unsure that either of them would be welcomed.

'Please do,' Robyn answered, recovering quickly from her initial shock. If she was to marry Julian, she did not want to be regarded badly by his family, despite the ill-feeling Janet had shown all those months ago. After all that had happened, that bitter encounter was best forgotten if Janet did not wish to remember it either.

At first the meeting was awkward, but the baby provided a focus that dispelled some of the embarrassment. Robyn offered her to Janet to hold, and the older woman sat with her, tears trickling down her cheeks as her heart opened up to her tiny granddaughter.

'I've been so afraid...I said such dreadful things to you, Robyn. Can you forgive me for being such a fool?' she asked, her eyes begging for a second chance.

Robyn remembered Julian saying that Janet had been out of her mind with grief, not responsible for her actions. 'In the circumstances it was understandable. But what you said wasn't true, Janet,' Robyn said quietly, wanting that to be clearly understood if there were to be any chance of effecting a real reconciliation.

'We know that, Robyn,' Wade answered for both of them. 'No one could have been more generous-hearted than you, and we both thank you, very sincerely, for having our granddaughter.'

'Davey...was so happy with her,' Janet said haltingly, her eyes weeping again as she spoke. 'It was a wonderful thing you did, Robyn. It was a wonderful thing to see. I'll never forget it.'

'I'm glad he lived long enough,' Robyn said softly.

'Yes. Yes, I'm glad too,' Janet said with a brave little smile.

'Robyn,' Wade Lassiter broke in, a plea in his eyes, 'we would like very much to be part of Faith's life. If you could find it in your heart to let us see you both from time to time...'

'Of course,' Robyn quickly agreed.

He smiled in relief. 'And Janet is a paediatrician. Retired from practice now, but if you ever have any worries about the baby, any problems, she's just a phone-call away.'

Robyn smiled. 'That's very kind, and I surely will avail myself of the offer. I'm not exactly experienced with babies, but I'm learning fast.'

'I'll be happy to give you any advice you want. Any time at all,' Janet said eagerly, and her gaze dropped lovingly to the soft bundle in her arms. 'Davey's hair was that same shade when he was born.'

Wade Lassiter grinned. 'And don't forget where he got it from, Janet. That little girl takes after her grandfather.' Robyn looked at him in surprise and he laughed. 'My hair might be white now, but it was bright red when I was a boy.'

'Did Julian inherit his black hair from his mother?'

'That's right.' He gripped Robyn's hand in deep gratitude. 'You're just as Julian said, a fine woman. I'm very proud to have your acquaintance, to have you as my daughter-in-law.'

'It works both ways, Mr Lassiter,' Robyn said happily. 'There's nothing like having close family. Julian taught me that.'

When the Lassiters finally took their leave, Robyn realised that a whole new life was opening up for her. She hoped that Wade and Janet would not be upset about her marriage to Julian. She was sure in her own mind that it was what David would have wanted, and she hoped they would see it that way and still welcome her into the family. There had been enough hurt.

Julian took Robyn and Faith home from the hospital. Robyn's mother was already there waiting, having offered to stay with Robyn for the first two weeks until she got used to caring for the baby. Marjorie Kent had met Julian at the hospital, and as he became a very frequent visitor to the house, she was most impressed with Faith's devoted uncle.

And he was far more of an uncle than a man in love with her, Robyn thought fretfully. Sometimes she caught him silently watching her and she could have sworn it was with a look of intense hunger; but he never embraced her or kissed her with any lover-like fervour, not even when her mother was out.

Robyn couldn't decide if he was determined not to rush her, or wary of what her physical reaction to him might be. Either way she found the situation disturbing and distressing. And it worsened during the third week when her mother had gone.

Julian did not relax at all in her company. He exuded tension and he evaded touching her at all except by accident. His manner was strained. Occasionally she glimpsed a tortured look in his eyes and it frightened her.

Did he love her? Really love her? Or was it just a mixture of guilty conscience and the vow to look after

David's daughter that drove him towards a marriage he didn't really want in his heart?

One evening he arrived early while she was still giving Faith her six o'clock feed. The baby cried at the interruption, and Robyn settled at the kitchen table to finish feeding her rather than go back upstairs. She quickly unbuttoned her blouse and pushed it aside and Faith greedily went on sucking.

Robyn glanced up to say something to Julian and found him staring at her bared breast; his face pale and strained, sheer anguish in his eyes.

'I left the evening newspaper in the car,' he said, and beat a swift retreat out of the house.

Tears sprang to Robyn's eyes. He didn't want to touch her. He didn't want to see her. Was it because he couldn't forget she had been David's wife? Would it always come between them? Was their marriage doomed before it had even begun?

Julian didn't return until she had taken Faith back up to the nursery. Robyn heard him come in as she settled the baby into the bassinet.

'Robyn?' he called up the stairs when he didn't find her.

'Down...in a minute,' she managed in a wobbly voice. She couldn't stop crying. It was no good. She couldn't marry him if he didn't want to make love to her. She moved quietly out of the nursery, closed the door and stepped across the landing to her own bedroom, not even glancing down the staircase. She needed to mop up her tears before facing Julian.

'Robyn?' There was an anxious note in his voice.

'I'm coming,' she choked out, and grabbed a handkerchief from the drawer in her dressing-table.

She heard his footsteps on the stairs and frantically tried to compose herself. It was impossible. He reached her doorway and the tears were still spilling down her cheeks. She rounded on him in abject despair.

'I can't marry you, Julian. You don't want me,' she blurted out.

'Don't want you!' he rasped. A turbulent range of emotions worked over his face. 'You think... I don't want you?'

'What else can I think?' Robyn cried. 'You can't bear to touch me or...'

He was across the room so quickly, she didn't have time to finish. She was swept into a crushing embrace, her head pressed hard on to his shoulder, his chest heaving against her tender breasts. His mouth scraped over her hair with hot, vehement kisses.

'Does this feel as if I can't bear to touch you?' he demanded hoarsely. 'I'm going mad from wanting you, Robyn. Every hour, every minute, every second I have to keep waiting is an agony.'

'I don't want you to wait,' she cried recklessly, hardly believing in his passion for her but exulting in it.

He groaned. 'I must. It means too much. When we're married...'

'No!' The protest burst from her throat. She pulled back from him, her eyes pleading for the truth. 'I need you now, Julian. If you love me...'

'Robyn.' His hands caught her face to still her speech. His throat moved convulsively. His eyes were agonised by the war between need and tortured doubts. 'If I start, I won't be able to stop.'

His fingers dragged at her cheeks as still he struggled for control. But she slid her arms around his back and pressed her body to his, and the last threads of his control snapped. His fingers raked through her hair and his mouth crashed down on hers in a passionate demand for all she would give him.

And Robyn exulted in every mad moment of his violent need for her: every drowning devouring kiss, the wild discarding of clothes, the possessive plunder of his hands as they crushed her flesh into his, the intense intimacy of his body moving over hers, the absolute moment of truth as he thrust inside her.

And it was the same, the same melting ecstasy and mindless craving for more and more until satiation was finally reached and drained slowly into blissful contentment. And again time had no meaning, ecstasy piled upon ecstasy, into a certainty that could never be denied!

They lay with their bodies entwined, just as they had done before on Maui, and the man in her arms was the same man. She knew every line of his powerful body, every muscle, every placement of bone, the touch of him, the scent of him, the texture of his flesh, the feel of his hair; impossible not to know.

It had been Julian all along. Hadn't she always known it at some instinctive level that she hadn't fully trusted? She still didn't know why or how, but he couldn't deny it now.

And it explained so much of what had happened: Julian's look of guilt and torment over the hurt he had given her, the haunted look, so full of painful regret, his anguish over David who had clung to life to see a child that was not his.

Faith was Julian's baby!

A thrill of happiness swept away all the pain he had iven her. W' .t did it matter now? Her baby—the baby

Julian had so desperately wanted to see born—was Julian's child! And Julian really did love both of them. She couldn't doubt it now.

Robyn recalled his incredulous delight when he had seen the colour of Faith's hair. What had he felt? That God had forgiven him the deception and even lent a hand to it—Dominique—a child of the Lord! The genes had not come from David but from Wade, grandfather to granddaughter. The atavistic characteristic coming through with a frequent enough occurrence in families.

And Julian's breaking down the night David died, grief riddled with the terrible guilt of months of needless suffering for his brother, because of the baby he himself had fathered.

Or had David known what Julian had done? How could he have been deceived? And yet all the evidence seemed to point the other way, that David had believed Faith was his child! And Julian saying he hoped it had been right for David, and determined on making it right for her! By marrying her!

He would try to deny it. She knew he would. Hadn't he already denied it when she had surprised him that third night in Maui? But she wouldn't let him get away with it this time.

There could be no holding back now. She couldn't risk Julian pulling away from her, not mentally, emotionally or physically. No matter what he had done, she loved him too much to lose him. But he had to tell her the truth now or there could never be total trust in their relationship.

'Julian...'

'Mmm?' His fingers grazed up and down her spine just as they had done so long ago.

She kissed him. Then softly, gently, she opened Pandora's box to the light of truth. 'David is dead, Julian, and the knowledge can't hurt him now. I know it was you who came to my bedroom at Maui. I know that you are our daughter's father. So please, don't deny it any longer. It doesn't make any difference to my loving you.'

His fingers were still. She felt the tension in his body, the sudden rapid beat of his heart, the slow, controlled expulsion of breath. 'This is madness, Robyn,' he said quickly, with attempted lightness. 'What on earth made you think of such a thing?'

And he moved, rolling her on to her back and propping himself up on his side to look down at her; instinctively putting himself in the dominant position. 'After all we've been through, you can't really believe that,' he said more forcefully.

Robyn could feel the fear behind his defence; the need to keep the status quo rather than risk a change he couldn't bear. She reached up and stroked his cheek to impart reassurance. 'Do you love me, Julian?' she asked softly.

'What more can I do to prove it to you?' he said huskily, turning his face to kiss the palm of her hand.

'Share this with me,' she pressed persuasively. 'Don't keep it to yourself, Julian. It's too late for that, and it can only hurt both of us if you persist in lying to me. I promise you it will always remain a secret between us. No one else need ever know.'

'Robyn...' It was a strangled cry of anguish. He leaned over and kissed her with a desperation that wanted to wipe everything else out of her mind. 'Don't do this!' he begged hoarsely. 'Leave it be, Robyn.'

'No. You've got to trust me, Julian,' she insisted, calmly and quietly relentless. It was impossible to retreat now, and she didn't want to. He had to trust her.

'How can you be so sure?' The words burst from him in pained protest.

'I'm not just sure, Julian. I'm certain.'

She felt him shudder. Then, with a groan, he rolled away from her. His legs swung out from the bedclothes and he sat hunched on the side of the bed, defeated by her denial of any doubt whatsoever.

'How long have you known?' His voice was edged with agonised despair.

Robyn hitched herself over to press herself against his back, anxious not to be separated from him in any way. 'I think I always knew,' she confided. 'But with certainty only when you made love to me just now.'

He shook his head in anguished defeat. 'How could I not make love to you? I've wanted, waited so long! I hoped the memory of how it had been might have diminished. But forgive me, Robyn. I know it's hardly possible, but at the time I thought it was the only way. And I love you, I love you so much.'

'And I love you,' she assured him, rubbing her cheek against his shoulder.

Another shudder shook his frame and he rose to his feet as if he couldn't bear her touch or dare to believe her words. 'How can you love me after all I've done?' he cried, and paced the room, too distraught to be still. 'Robyn, I know I deceived you, but never again. Never! Never! I swear to you I'll spend my whole life making up for the pain and agony I've caused you. I can't live without you, Robyn. Please don't send me away. What can I do?'

'I have no intention of sending you away, Julian,' Robyn cried out, desperate to appease his anguish. 'I won't ever do that. All I want is to know why. I want to understand. I realise that you must have done it for your brother, but why did you take David's place?'

He paused and took a deep breath. 'I found out—after the wedding—that Davey was sterile.'

After the wedding...after all the decisions had been made and arrangements agreed to, the whole commitment already in train.

'The laboratory accident caused more damage than Davey knew.' Julian gestured helplessly and moved over to the window, pushing aside the curtains so that he could look out, look anywhere but at Robyn. But the moonlight that streamed in was merciless, turning his face into a marble cast of suffering.

'You remember he was donating his life to science.' The words were pushed out with difficulty. 'Something prompted me, I don't know what. I rang the university. I hadn't thought of it before. I suddenly had this premonition and felt forced to act on it. They told me that he was sterile. There was nothing anyone could do. Afterwards I made them promise never to reveal the truth to him.'

Robyn could see the harrowed look on his face, his agony of mind, his guilt.

He shook his head. 'At the time I went to tell him, to tell him that we had to call the whole thing off, and I couldn't do it. He was so happy, bubbling with happiness. And then I found out that he expected the baby to be conceived by artificial insemination.'

'What?' Robyn couldn't help the shocked squeak.

Julian sighed and turned to her. 'Robyn, I hadn't even thought of the possibility when I was making all the arrangements with you. Davey was the scientist. And you hadn't put it into the conditions. It came as a shock to me too, but it seeded the mad scheme that grew in my mind. At first I tossed it out as horrendous. But it was possible, you see, if I was ruthless enough. To pretend to Davey that I would take the sample to you.'

'And use my key and the darkness I insisted upon to do what I expected,' Robyn finished for him, seeing precisely how her conditions had bolstered the temptation.

'I didn't stop to think, to work it all out, it was purely instinct. I would pretend to be Davey, and when you were pregnant he would think it was his baby, and he would be happy. At the time, I would have done anything—almost anything—to make him happy.' His face contorted with guilty anguish. 'So I did this horrendous thing to you. You must think me a monster, the most despicable, contemptible...'

'No, Julian! I can see you did it from need and love and...'

'But the pain I've caused you, all the misery and agony of mind and body. How can I ever make it up to you?'

'With a lifetime of loving,' Robyn answered promptly and firmly, and it took his breath away.

He stared at her, struggling to believe, needing desperately to believe. 'You can still love me, even knowing what I did?'

'Julian, I know you did it out of love for David. And I know you love me now. And our child. Do you honestly think I would throw away something so precious?' she reasoned more gently. 'Please, come back to me now,

Julian. I want you to hold me and love me as I know you always will.'

He was at her side in a few swift strides and he swept her out of the bed and into his arms, crushing her to him as he smothered her face and hair with kisses and fevered words that carried a torrent of emotion.

'Oh, Robyn, my Robyn, I do love you. I love you so much, I can't bear to live without you. I thought if I told you what I did, you would hate me for ever. And I would have deserved it, just as I deserved it when you sent me away and said you never wanted to see me again. You did right. You were too good for me, so beautiful and loving and . . . it was the first time in my life I felt despair.'

'You loved me then, Julian?' Robyn asked in incredulous wonder.

'My darling, I was falling in love with you from the moment we met,' he said apologetically. 'It accelerated when you first gave me your answer for Davey. I couldn't hold on to my dislike of women—the deep resentment I had from what my wife had chosen to do. She . . .'

'I know about Vanessa, Julian. Tina told me,' Robyn put in quickly.

'She promised me everything, Robyn, and gave nothing. Vanessa only ever thought of herself. I hoped after the accident that starting a family might help her to adjust, give her another interest, children of her own to love. I knew my love wasn't enough to console her. But she destroyed herself rather than accept a life she didn't want.'

He dragged in a deep breath and the old bitterness was swallowed up in a blaze of need for her. 'I didn't know what a woman could be like until I met you, my darling. You were so wonderful, so giving, and when I came to you as Davey... I knew then what perfection in a woman could do to a man.'

He sighed and swept his cheek across her hair in yearning love for her. 'But the reckoning came, Robyn. The bliss of realising that I loved you was needled with the agony of thinking you had fallen in love with Davey. I was at the point of madness when I came to you that third night, racked with guilt and jealousy and desire, and you were right to make me pay for what I'd done. But, Robyn, I've got to confess, I wanted you to have my child. I was hanging on to that hope as the only line I had to get back into your life.'

'I'm glad...that it wasn't only for David,' she said on a wave of huge relief. 'I wished it could be your baby even before I agreed to marry him, Julian. I did what you asked of me, because you asked it. I needed you in my life. I knew I loved you even as I married your brother. It was you I made love with. Only ever you in my mind. I didn't know how or why, and when you denied it, I died inside. I couldn't bear to see you again. I wanted you as I could never want your brother.'

Again his eyes begged her forgiveness. 'Robyn, believe me, it was hell for me too, knowing that I'd trapped us both into a situation that seemed endless, and watching Davey hold on by inches.'

He shuddered and she held him close. 'David loved you,' she said softly, remembering their greeting at the Hyatt-Regency on Maui, and David's saying how wonderful it was to see Julian with a woman again—hope for the future. And the future was assured now. 'He would have suffered to see you happy, just as you did for him, Julian.'

'I don't know, Robyn,' he said with infinite sadness. 'I'll never know.'

She reached up and held his face, urging her own deeply held conviction. 'You think he isn't smiling at us now? He gave me into your keeping, Julian. And he wanted you to have the baby, to look after and love. He wanted us to have each other.'

A sudden flash of insight drew another picture—one she hadn't thought of before—but it felt so right she had no hesitation in putting it into words.

'You said David had a brilliant analytical mind. Couldn't he have worked it all out for your sake, Julian? I'm not saying he didn't want a child of his own, but he was leaving the child to you—someone to love who would take his place in your life. A life you once told me was meaningless. Don't you think he knew that? That he wanted it to be different for you?'

She saw the considering look in Julian's eyes and rushed on. 'David said how much you had always done for him. What was the best thing he could do for you before he died, Julian? Wouldn't it be something to give your life meaning, to make you happy? Faith and I, we're his legacy to you. His hope for your future happiness. Doesn't that sound right to you?'

The shadow of torment was cleared from his eyes by a blaze of love. He stroked her face with the touch of reverence. 'If Davey chose you for me, he could not have been more right. You're an amazing person, Robyn Lassiter.'

And this time, the Lassiter name sounded as if it had been made for her. 'I think that our daughter is blessed with an amazing father. And in a way, Faith is David's daughter, too. She was conceived because he wanted her, because he chose me as her mother, because you loved him, Julian. Without David, she wouldn't have been born.' She smiled. 'And he loved her as much as we do.'

Julian relaxed and smiled back at her. 'Yes. But I must confess to you, my darling, that I don't think Faith will become a scientific genius. That talent comes from Janet's side of the family. So I'm afraid it's most unlikely she will ever win a Nobel Prize.'

'What does it matter?' Robyn sighed contentedly. 'If she inherits your genius for loving, the world won't lose by it. That's the most important thing of all, Julian. Loving.'

It was true. What was a life worth if there was no love in it? And without David's love for his brother, Julian's love for him, his love for her, they would never have found each other; and Faith would never have been born.

The old lady had been right.

The greatest sadness...

And then the greatest happiness.

But through it all, it was the loving that was important.

Harlequin Presents.

Coming Next Month

Available in October wherever paperback books are sold, or through Harlequin Reader Service:

In the U.S.
901 Fuhrmann Blvd.
P.O. Box 1397
Buffalo, N.Y. 14240-1397

In Canada
P.O. Box 603
Fort Erie, Ontario
L2A 5X3

Have You Ever Wondered If You Could Write A Harlequin Novel?

Here's great news—Harlequin is offering a series of cassette tapes to help you do just that. Written by Harlequin editors, these tapes give practical advice on how to make your characters—and your story—come alive. There's a tape for each contemporary romance series Harlequin publishes.

Mail order only

All sales final